FILTHY NEIGHBOR

A BAD BOY NEXT DOOR ROMANCE

SCARLETT KING

HOT AND STEAMY ROMANCE

CONTENTS

Sign Up to Receive Free Books	v
Blurb	vii
1. Tina	1
2. Tina	6
3. Jimmy	12
4. Tina	17
5. Jimmy	22
6. Tina	27
7. Jimmy	32
8. Tina	41
9. Jimmy	47
10. Tina	53
11. Jimmy	59
12. Tina	65
13. Jimmy	69
14. Tina	73
Sign Up to Receive Free Books	77
Preview of The Promise of Love	79
Chapter one	81
Chapter Two	88
Chapter Three	104
Chapter Four	118
Other Books By This Author	125
Copyright	127

Made in "The United States" by:

Scarlett King

© Copyright 2020 – Scarlett King

ISBN: ISBN: 978-1-64808-025-8

ALL RIGHTS RESERVED. No part of this publication may be reproduced or transmitted in any form whatsoever, electronic, or mechanical, including photocopying, recording, or by any informational storage or retrieval system without express written, dated and signed permission from the author

❦ Created with Vellum

SIGN UP TO RECEIVE FREE BOOKS

Sign Up to Receive Free E-Books and Audiobook Codes.

Would you like to read **The Unexpected Nanny, Dirty Little Virgin** and **other romance books** for **free?**

You can sign up to receive these free e-books and audiobooks by typing this link into your browser:

https://www.steamyromance.info/free-books-and-audiobooks-hot-and-steamy/

Or this one:

https://www.steamyromance.info/the-unexpected-nanny-free/

BLURB

Virginal, shy loner Tina thinks that all she can do is look when she gets a crush on her hot, mysterious neighbor Jimmy. But Jimmy's noticed her looking, and he likes what he sees as well. As things heat up between them, she has no idea that Jimmy's got an ulterior motive. Naughty Jimmy's leading a double life, and he may like Tina, but he's also seducing her to make sure she doesn't see more than she's supposed to. But when a stroke of bad luck brings her face to face with his dark, criminal world, Jimmy must make a choice. Can he trust he to keep his secret, or does she have to die?

Tina

I want him, but all I can do is look.

My new neighbor Jimmy is the hottest guy I've ever seen, and I can't take my eyes off him, but I'm untouched, inexperienced; I've barely even dated, and I have no idea what being with a man would even be like. I want Jimmy to teach me, but how do I even approach a stud like him without seeming like a fool?

Jimmy

The little cutie next door is spying on me. She watches me when I exercise. She watches me when I use my hot tub and when I take a lover into it. It's clearly a crush—and I like it. Those bright, longing eyes of hers turn me on. They make me want to show her that some things are much more fun to do than watch. There's just one problem—if she's been watching me, she may have seen too much. I'm a problem-solver for my uncle Ezio, the local mob boss. I leave at odd hours. I keep odd company. One day, she may figure it out. And if that happens, I have to make sure she's already too attached to me to give me up to the cops. But there's a simple solution. The little lady has a crush. She wants me to show her what it's all about in bed. And with my secrecy at stake, I have to ask: why not give her what she wants?

1

TINA

Sitting in my new sun room deleting the morning crop of dick pics off my Instagram DMs, I hear the back door of my neighbor's brownstone slam. My heart leaps. It's seven in the morning, the sun is lighting the Brooklyn rooftops pink and gold, and my favorite morning show is about to start.

Jimmy is all the reason I need to get up early, like he does every day like clockwork. The only time he doesn't is when he's out of town—and those days, I don't bother getting up before nine. But most days, the extra sleepiness is worth it, just for the chance to watch him at his morning routine. He goes out into his immaculate garden with the lush fruit trees, hot tub, and perfectly manicured lawn, takes off his robe, and works out wearing nothing but a pair of black boxer briefs.

I have no idea what this guy does in winter. I've only been here since April, after my Grandma's estate settled and I was able to move in. I discovered him early on, after spying his amazing gardening work from my attic bedroom window early one morning. And then he walked out his back door, dropped the robe, and left me staring at him nonstop for the next half hour.

Jimmy is the kind of guy I only watch from afar, longingly, too shy to go near. Huge, fit, handsome, intense, completely in control of his life and his powerful body—he looks like a Roman statue of Mars, except a lot better hung. From the sheer volume in the front of those briefs, in fact, it's either that, or he's smuggling a sleeping python. And the rest of him is just as captivating.

He's got those Mediterranean good looks that are just boyish enough to keep a guy his size from looking like a brute: Wavy, coffee-colored hair, smooth olive skin, and deep black eyes. I looked into those eyes once, when we introduced ourselves, and felt as dizzy and weak-kneed as if I was about to go tumbling into them.

He dresses well, too—understated suits, tailored leather blazers, and if he's wearing jeans, they're cut to show off those muscular legs, his sculpted ass, and that hefty bulge in front. I found him attractive with his clothes on, but when I finally saw him stripped down for exercise in the garden, I was hooked for good.

It's only gotten worse since then. I dream of him at night. I spy on him by day, watching him exercise, tend to his garden, and soak in the hot tub. I try to push myself to talk to him again, to find some excuse to start doing so regularly, but I just don't have the nerve.

What would a guy like that ever want with a hopeless virgin anyway?

All my experiences of love and sex have been negative. I haven't even tried dating since I went out on my own at eighteen, so I have no idea what to do. I know I will mess things up with Jimmy if I approach him. So instead, I watch, and I dream, and I wonder if I'm a pervert or just a coward. I can't stop. Looking at him now, though, I think, Who would want to?

He's doing push-ups now, his back muscles gleaming in the

thin sunlight as they flex, warming up. I watch the tight mounds of his ass move up and down, more decorated than clothed by the clinging black fabric, and imagine what it would be like to be pinned under his heavy, hot body. And I wish, like I do every damn morning, that I was just a little bit braver.

My therapist at the Center would tell me to go talk to him. My therapist at the Center—currently a delicate-featured Indian man who looks more like a kindergarten teacher than someone sent to evaluate my sanity—would ask me why I haven't dated and suggest again that I'm not as recovered as I like to think. My therapist, however, is an idiot. Not everything can be chalked up to trauma.

Some of it is a simple matter of male courtship skills not being what they used to be, which is a very kind way of saying that nine out of ten guys who show an interest in me open a conversation with something on the level of "Trynna fuck?" and send pictures of their dicks within five minutes. Apparently, that's just to be expected these days.

I want none of it. I want romance. I want seduction. I want something good after all the bad in my life, and I've saved myself for it. I want...him.

Jimmy moved to work on his pull-up bar, his soft grunts of effort reaching my ears through the open window. The cool morning air smells of flowers, mixing with the taste of my green tea and the faint musk of my aroused body as I watch him. Every time he hauls his body up by the arms and chins over the bar, I feel a catch in my chest. He's a different breed from twenty-something fuckboys or older predators. He wouldn't hassle me like the way I'm being hassled daily. I know he wouldn't.

It's not just my dating account, which I gave up on a month ago from sheer frustration. Men hit me up on my Facebook, on gaming accounts, and of course, on my business website and its connected Instagram. Every single damn morning, I end up going through and deleting vulgar sexual overtures and unwanted pictures of ugly cocks, sometimes with leering faces behind them. I don't want a man like that. And they're everywhere. I don't have the endurance for the frog-kissing phase of dating life.

Jimmy's doing crunches on his slant board now, sweat glistening over his rippling abs and shoulders. I lick my lips, my mouth suddenly dry. I wonder if he's seeing anyone. I never see him with any given woman more than once. But even if I am a great spy, it doesn't mean I know everything about him. Still, what a mystery to investigate, especially if it gets my mind off crap like what's on my screen.

My Instagram has absolutely nothing sexual on it. It is of home renovation projects—jobs done by my fledgling company, Carson Renovations. I am currently living in our first big project—my Grandmother's brownstone, willed to me along with the seed money for my business. Grandma always came through for me. She was the only one in my whole damned family who ever did.

The only images of me online are about as sexy as graph paper. Me in a loose, paint-splattered coverall, red hair tucked under a hard hat, and blue eyes hidden behind safety goggles, pointing out things to my crew, helping to strip wallpaper, reading renovation plans, but it doesn't matter. I still get nonsense in my inboxes.

As I dig through my email and direct messages looking for serious inquiries and work opportunities, I delete four more dick pics, two requests for sex, one tantrum from a guy who keeps making new accounts to harass me from, and six marriage proposals from Nigerian romance scammers. Whyyyy? What did I do to deserve this?

I look away from my phone, back down to the yard where the man I wish I could make notice me is doing martial arts katas of some kind all over his lawn. I watch him kick above his head, do splits, and practice strikes on an odd-looking wooden dummy he fashioned from a log. If I wasn't so enthralled with him, I would be frightened.

He could break me like a twig. But somehow, that just makes things hotter. Especially if he cares enough to hold his strength in check...at least, until he can't anymore.

It's been a long time since I looked at a man and liked what I saw enough to wonder what sex with him would be like. Now, I drink Jimmy in, and I do more than wonder. I crave it, but I don't know how to approach him.

What the hell am I going to do?

2

TINA

It's been a long, frustrating day. My kitchen is still in pieces. I'm blowing money on takeout every night that I can't afford, and everyday there's been a new setback. Today, the range hood delivery was delayed, we ran out of tiles nine-tenths of the way through covering the floor thanks to two missing boxes, and my business number got an obscene phone call. Now, at least the floor is done, and the caller is blocked. I'm ready to sleep almost right away.

I force myself to eat some melon and cottage cheese from the office fridge I set up in the corner of my finished master bedroom. I shower off the dust and grime and wrap myself in a white silk robe, one of my few luxuries. Then, I glance out the window.

The lights are on at Jimmy's place, and so far, he's not using his hot tub; his beautiful back yard is dark. I saw him bring some blonde inside when we came back from buying more tile and had to fight down jealousy. He's in there with her now, this anonymous bitch, the luckiest woman in the world.

I pour myself enough scotch over ice to make the bitterness go away, swallow it like medicine, and go to bed early.

There's a shadow outside the window that shouldn't be there.

The neighborhood lives under a blanket of fear at night. Mom and Dad and all the other moms and dads hide their kids away the moment the sun goes down. They draw their shades, lock doors and windows, and check on them ten times a night.

Four kids have vanished in the last two months. Their bodies always turn up in the woods. Things are done to them, things that my parents won't tell me about.

The kids in that neighborhood whisper together in the schoolyard every break and at lunch. It's a man in a wolf mask, they say. He takes kids away—young, like us, like me at ten, untouched yet by puberty. The man in the wolf mask does things to those kids, and then kills them.

The kids from our neighborhood talk at lunch about who it might be. They think it's one of the grownups who lives here —but who?

We also talk about the weapons we keep under our pillows to keep us and our younger siblings safe. One of us steals a knife from the block in the kitchen every night. Another sleeps with a baseball bat. Yet another was given a screamer alarm by her mother and scared herself out of her socks setting it off when she rolled over on it at night. Not me, I can beat them all.

I know where Daddy keeps his gun.

I don't like sleeping with a pistol tucked into my nightstand drawer, but I know Daddy won't protect me if the man in the wolf mask comes. Once my cold, distant parents warn me about something, I'm the one who is expected to avoid it. They don't like repeating themselves. Especially Daddy. So every night after they are asleep, I take the gun from his desk drawer and put it in my nightstand drawer. And every morning before they wake up, I bring it back.

Daddy got drunk once and showed me how to take the safety

off, how to hold it, and how to keep my finger off the trigger until I'm ready to fire. Daddy sleeps with Mommy on another floor of the sprawling, old house, and I know he will not come if I scream for help, so I have his gun instead of him.

And now there is a shadow outside my window that should not be there.

I quietly pull the drawer open in the dark and fish the pistol out. It feels heavy and cold in my hand.

I sit up with a gasp, the warm night air mixing weirdly with the cold sweat all over my skin. Catching my breath, I look around at my airy bedroom with its bank of windows, the gauze curtains blowing softly in the slight breeze, and relax. At least these days my flashbacks only happen in dreams.

I am trying to pull myself together when I hear something outside the window: a low, cooing moan. It repeats after a few moments, and then dissolves into rhythmic panting. Frowning, I pull my robe around me and move to the window, looking around for the source of the sound.

Jimmy's garden glows softly with the strings of fairy lights he ran over the fences and some of the bushes and trees. A few paper lanterns shine their white-gold radiance over the small deck where Jimmy has his jacuzzi. I can't quite see—the view from my bedroom isn't as good as from the sun room—but I can tell that the jacuzzi is occupied.

"Don't stop," croons a female voice. I feel a flash of jealousy even as my skin starts to tingle. "Don't stop. Oh God, that's good. Ohhh God...."

I hurry across to the sun room and pull aside the curtains. The windows are already open. My phobia isn't so bad anymore that I worry about open windows as long as they are well above ground level. The attic bedroom and its adjoining sun room can't be reached from the outside by anyone short of a mountain climber. I just remind myself of that fact whenever my nerves start acting up.

My eyes fix on the scene in the jacuzzi and widen as my heart starts to pound. Oh God, that lucky, lucky bitch.

I can't even see the woman in question; Jimmy's crouched over her against the side of the jacuzzi, his big body blocking hers from sight. Now and again, I see a hand clutching at him, or a pale knee break the surface of the water, but that barely registers as I drink Jimmy in.

He is nude, bathing suit shoved down his thighs, and his bare ass clenches as he rolls his hips in the frothy water. He isn't speaking save for the occasional grunt; I suspect his mouth is busy...doing things to her. The whole thought of that makes my cheeks burn and heat gather between my untouched thighs.

He strains and grinds against the unseen woman, one of his hands busy between them while the other braces him above her. His muscles bulge tautly under his gleaming skin, the strain of holding back showing in every line of his body as he pleasures her.

Her voice almost sounds like she is in pain. "Ah...ah...ahhhh don't stop...yes...just like that...yes...oh...I'm gonna—!"

I listen, more fascinated than jealous now. What does that feel like?

A moment later, I hear long, muffled wails as he quiets her with a kiss. And again, I wonder.

I have never had sex. I have also never had an orgasm. I've always been pretty body shy; I don't masturbate, and the few boys I briefly dated couldn't have found my clit with a map and a miner's light.

I have heard orgasms described. I have heard people having them. But never me. I don't really understand what could possibly feel so good as to make a woman scream out and wake up the neighbors in the middle of the night.

I want to find out. With Jimmy. Nobody else.

"My turn, baby," he says hoarsely, lifting his head.

I hurry to the far end of the sun room, peeking through the curtains, trying to get a better look at his profile instead of just that magnificent ass pumping away, though that isn't a bad vision. I want to see his face right now. I'm rewarded by an eyeful of the whole sculpted line of his body, every muscle taut with excitement as he speeds his thrusts.

I stare, fascinated. I can see everything. Unfortunately, I see a bit too much of the blonde; I can see the line of her thigh, one arm clutched around his back...but the rest is worth it.

His face is creased with pleasure, lips parted, eyes closed as he pumps his cock into her in ever faster and harder strokes. I see his condom-wrapped shaft vanishing into her again and again. Thick, glistening. Every time he sinks into her, they shudder like they're on the brink of something overwhelming.

He starts to lose control, his grunts becoming audible as he fucks her roughly, then lengthening to hoarse groans and shouts. He pushes her up onto the edge of the jacuzzi and climbs halfway out, gripping her hips as he keeps pounding away.

His expression shifts from strained to blissful and back as he thrusts. She starts moaning again, and he choruses with her while his ass flexes and his hips bound against her like he's trying to drive his cock right through her.

I press my knees together, watching him creep up to the edge of something foreign to me, and try to imagine myself under him again. His back arches, his head falls back, and his shouts gain intensity until he goes completely hoarse.

"Come on, Jimmy," I murmur as I watch him race to the finish. "Come on. Let go. Come on, baby."

He goes rigid except for his fiercely rolling hips, eyes flying open and going wide. His back arches harder—and then a long groan echoes through the yard.

I smile, full of sadness and desire and desperate curiosity, and move away from the window as he collapses over her. Oh, Jimmy, I think wistfully, knowing that I'll never get back to sleep now. I wish you were doing that with me instead.

I have to find some excuse to talk to him. Something interesting. Something we have in common. I have no idea how to flirt, but I can start there.

3

JIMMY

I cum nice and hard into Mrs. Torrington , whose husband I am going to kill later tonight, and all my stress roars out of me with my load. I sigh with relief and let myself relax over her a moment, reveling in my body's bliss. It's the only time I'm awake that I can ever really take it easy—those precious few post-sex minutes when I can rest in a woman's arms.

But then the hollowness comes back, and I'm reminded that I'm actually alone, and that none of them are mine. Or even worth making mine.

Mrs. Torrington—Marie, that's her first name, better not slip up on that—lounges nude on a towel on my deck, whole body slack, practically purring. She's a hot blonde in her late thirties, maybe five years older than me, and from the way she's reacting, she hasn't had a proper fuck in years. Apparently the soon-to-be-late Mr. Torrington has been neglecting his duties.

She's so drowsy, in fact, that I almost don't have to use the drug, but I know better than to risk it. I need her out for an hour while I do my job, and even my dick can't guarantee that. The syringe is tiny, hidden inside the leather bracer on my left wrist.

Its needle is so thin she doesn't even twitch when I slide it under her skin.

Tonight, Mrs. Torrington is my toy, my way of getting into her house...and also, my alibi. She's likely going to wake up a widow tomorrow morning, though she has no idea.

I smooth her tangled blonde hair back from her sleeping face and scoop her up to carry her inside. I can tuck her into the guest room bed and come back from the job to fuck her some more, making her think I've just been curled up with her, waiting for her to recover the whole time.

As I do, I glance up and see the curtains of my neighbor's third-floor sun room twitch slightly. I have to fight down a grin. Did you enjoy the show, shy girl?

Some women have a Peeping Tom. I have a Peeping Tina. I'm a lot luckier than those ladies, who generally have to get a restraining order against some mouth-breathing creep who gets off on their discomfort as much as his invasion of their privacy. It's a lot less threatening to have a cute, shy, virginal young woman watching you longingly whenever she thinks you won't notice.

That adorable little hottie of a neighbor means me no harm at all. Far from it actually; her crush on me is clearly already so huge that it makes me smile to think about it. Tina really is just fucking cute, and the way she looks at me is a bright spot in my often dark and ugly world.

I've left her alone because I don't want to pull her into that world, my world. She might get hurt. But God, I'd love to make every little daydream she's ever had about me come true. There's just one problem, and I mull it over as I carry Mrs. Torrington inside: my little Peeping Tina has already seen too much.

I lay Mrs. Torrington in the bed and go into the living room where she left her purse. Her third highball has melted into a diluted mess of booze-flavored ice water on the coffee table next to it. Seducing her into betraying her husband barely took any effort, and now her guilt over it will keep her mouth shut about it forever.

Still just in my shorts, I grab a pair of black latex gloves from a box in the coffee table drawer and pull them on before opening her purse. I have a job to do. The problem is, Tina's likely to notice me leaving. The poor girl's obsessed. Even if she isn't actively watching, I know she'll register the engine noise.

Still, by the time I'm done, absolutely no one will be able to tie me to this job. In fact, they probably won't realize that it's a hit at all unless the coroner's a damn genius. Greg Torrington didn't hurt anybody; he just knows too much about my boss's operations and doesn't know how to keep his mouth shut, so he gets to die in his sleep.

I did my homework. He's sixty-eight, drinks hard, and has a heart condition that he does nothing for. It will take the tiniest dose of the right sedatives to put him in a coma from heart failure. Marie will come home tingling all over from the best sex of her life, take a guilty shower, and lie down next to a guy who will never wake up. Her morning won't be pleasant, even if he survives long enough for a stay on life-support, but it's not like she won't have expected it—and in the end, it's to her benefit. She married him for his money, after all.

But Tina will have seen Mrs. Torrington here, and Torrington is rich. His death will make the news. Tina's not stupid. If she recognizes my target's wife, the timing of our "date" will make her curious.

I open the purse and pull out Marie's keys and cell phone after digging for it. She has her "smart" house lights, cameras and alarm on remote, and as soon as I crack her screen lock password, the system is mine. I notice immediately that she already has the house cameras turned off so that her husband, who likely drank himself to sleep hours before, would not have a record of her sneaking out. How convenient. Now they won't have a record of me sneaking in either.

I dress in a nondescript dark blue track suit and matching hoodie, complete with a pair of jogger's headphones and track shoes as camouflage. The whole time, my mind is wandering from the job to shy, hard-working little Tina, whom I'd love to seduce.

The thought of her is enough to make my dick stir awake after two bouts of sex. I don't really know what her story is. After the old lady next door died, the place went empty for a while—and then, a few months ago, Tina moved in. She's been fixing the place up ever since. She has a crew of three guys, and gets down and dirty herself handling it all. But other than fixing things and running errands, she doesn't seem to have a life.

Sometimes, in the middle of the night, I hear her scream out suddenly, and then start crying. I think she has nightmares. Poor little thing.

What the fuck happened to her? I wonder as I finish looking through Marie's purse. I leave it exactly where it was sitting, careful to put everything back inside as I found it—except for her keys and phone. Those I'll replace before I wake her up with more sex. I can already tell I'll be thinking about my little Peeping Tina again when I fuck Marie. I don't think I would have blown my load half as hard if I had not known that she was watching.

As I'm on my way down the stairs to take the Torrington car out to their mansion on East 62nd, I feel that tug of worry again. At what point will little, virgin Tina become a liability from watching me so much? And what the hell do I do about it?

Then it dawns on me, and I can't help but grin as I pull out onto the road. If I want Tina distracted, attached to me, and willing to do almost anything to keep me out of trouble, the answer's easy...and fun, too. Why not give the lady what she wants?

4

TINA

Thursday morning is therapy morning. I'm down to only once a week now. Good thing too, because all it really does anymore is remind me of the past. And I would really rather move on. Thinking about things from your childhood over and over is more than a hindrance than it is help.

Dr. Singh sits in his chair with his ankle on his knee, and his big brown eyes full of confusion. "You're telling me that you have met someone, but you have not actually...gone on a date or anything? Is this 'meeting someone,' or is it just a crush?"

Ugh, fuck you, Doc. "It's not just a crush. I have talked to him, I just haven't...gotten that far." And probably never will, but that's not his business. He's the one saying that I need to try dating again. He's not the one clearing dick pics off his phone every morning or living with my memories.

He frowns and sets both feet on the floor, leaning forward. He has slim little hands that he steeples as he considers me. "It does sound like progress, but only token progress. And only in the one area. I should ask...how are your dreams this week?"

I sigh and sit back, looking away from him, out the window.

They're digging up the street outside his office, and the noise of asphalt being cut whines through my temples. "I'd rather talk about Jimmy."

No, that's not accurate. I'd rather not be here at all. But he doesn't need to know that. Dr. Singh is a kind person who means well, unlike other therapists I have had over the years. He will be genuinely hurt if I tell him just how useless I feel that our sessions are.

He's not a bad shrink, but it's been over ten years. I've been a legal adult for almost three. If talking about this crap was going to make it go away, it would have left by now, right?

"Well, I guess that makes sense. A crush is a much more pleasant topic than post-traumatic stress." He smiles a little indulgently. But I know what's coming and am not even surprised when he goes on with "But I still have to ask."

I roll my eyes. "Yes, I'm still having nightmares. Yes, I still check the windows on the ground floor several times a night."

He makes a note. "Just the ground floor windows now?"

I blink at him, puzzled, then realize that I never told him that I finally talked myself out of sealing myself off in a stuffy house all summer. "Yeah. I can leave the upper windows open at night. I've been at it for a few weeks now. Sorry, thought I mentioned it."

He taps his lips with one finger, and then looks at me with a touch of regret in his eyes. "I need to ask about the dreams. About the story that they always tell. Your...memory of that night. You said that you can remember the ending now."

I seize up inside, but take a deep breath and try to work through it. I can remember the ending, all right. It involves me putting a bullet into the Wolf's Head Killer at the age of ten. "I shot the guy in the wolf mask when he broke into my room. I told him to leave me alone, and he wouldn't, so I shot him."

"Do you remember who he was?" he asked very gently. The question stopped me cold.

"Yeah," I sighed finally. "I remember." Of course I did. I hadn't at first, not for years. I hadn't understood why I spent eight years "away," why the courts wanted to try me as an adult, why so many hated me for defending myself. Why my mother, who should have protected me, hates me to this day. Now I do. And I think everyone who hates me for what I did is full of crap.

I killed a monster. It just so happened that the monster was my father. That was the face under the wolf mask, staring back at me in a frozen look of surprise as the police pulled it off him like a horrible version of Scooby-Doo.

At first, everyone insisted that my father had played a "prank" which had backfired horribly. Then the DNA evidence came back, and suddenly everyone knew that it was my father who had killed four kids after raping them. And that my father had planned to do the same to me.

Self-defense was a lot easier to prove after that, and I was found innocent of all charges, but the courts still stuck me in the damn nut house. My mother, a little too eager to be rid of me, simply never came to get me. My grandmother wrote me until she got too sick, but died before I was released at age eighteen. Though it took almost three years of legal wrangling with my mother, Grandma made sure that I had something to build a future from.

"Do you want to tell me how it's supposed to help me?" I ask suddenly, knowing it is probably pointless, but starting to get frustrated.

Dr. Singh frowns. "Sorry, what do you mean?"

"I mean, how is talking about the same bad memories over and over supposed to help me? Nobody's ever explained that part to me." I stare out the window at the sun climbing out from behind the buildings and close my eyes. I suddenly just want to be home. On familiar ground...and close to Jimmy.

"I know it's uncomfortable. But processing these emotions—" His voice has filled with worry. He knows how I get when I'm irritated enough.

I waved a hand in irritation. "Screw processing emotions. Look. There is no good way to feel about the fact that my father was a monster and that I had to shoot him in self-defense. If I had not shot him, I would have been victim number five. My father was a monster, and my mother was, and still is, a soulless bitch. The only one who ever loved me was Grandma, and I owe her everything. The rest of them, I don't owe shit."

"I understand that you have sorted out your emotions in healthier ways. But you can't tell me it doesn't make you sad not to have had a real relationship with your parents." He's taking notes. I hate it when he does that. It reminds me that I'm under a court order, and that my freedom could be at stake.

"Sometimes. But those feelings are pointless. I can grieve all I fucking want for the family I never really had, but that won't help me now. I would rather move on." I manage to keep my voice even, but his eyes go wide anyway.

"Are you asserting that you have somehow recovered because you have learned to cut your parents off emotionally?" He readjusts his glasses on his nose.

"I'm saying that if I have to go to therapy, I'd like to spend the time working on something that will help me more than rehashing the worst night of my life." I give him a pleading look, hoping that it will soften my words a little.

He sighs and finally nods. "All right, we'll try that. So about this Jimmy person. How much do you really know about him?"

I smile. "Not much yet. But I want to know everything."

For once, I don't feel sick when I leave my therapy session. If I had, it wouldn't have been Dr. Singh's fault; the subject matter has done it to me every time before now. But today: no queasiness, no urges to weep or hide. I am a little tired, but that is all.

I pull up outside my brownstone when I notice a familiar tall figure leaning in its doorway at the top of the brick stairs. I park, get out and lock up, then turn to move tentatively up the steps.

Jimmy smiles and straightens up to greet me, his dark eyes drawing me into their depths again. "Hey there, Tina," he says in a friendly tone that makes me warm all over. "I noticed that your kitchen's still in pieces. I prepped too much barbecue stuff for just me. You're welcome if you want to pop over and have some."

I stare. He flashes a grin at my surprise and waits. Finally, I just blink up at him and offer a tentative smile.

"Sure," I say, my heart pounding in my ears. "That sounds great."

5

JIMMY

The barbecue was a damn good idea. I know Tina loves my yard. It's the first thing she ever talked to me about. She asked me in her stumbly way whether I had ever worked with any renovation companies and offered the idea of us collaborating. I needed to tiptoe around that idea because the real job doesn't leave that much time for the cover job. Though at the end of the day, I'm great at both.

But now, I'm ready to talk it over with her again. Or really talk about anything else that gives me an excuse to get close to her. I'm not picky about subject matter.

She changed before coming, and her loose purple gauze dress clings to her as the wind blows it against her body. A little perfume wafts toward me now and again. It's a soft fragrance, one that suits her shyness. I let myself look at her as much as I want, already knowing she'll be into it. She notices my eyes roaming over her, and lowers her eyelashes demurely—peeping at me through them. Just adorable.

This one's special. I can tell already. One shy, heated look from her does more for me than a hand on my cock. The prospect of actually fucking her makes me ache with anticipation.

It almost feels...dangerous. Like I might lose control of my feelings. But I shake that worry off after a moment, amused at myself. I'm not about to let emotional risk scare me off of the fun of wrapping this little sweetie around my finger.

I've gone for gunshow in black jeans and a matching tank top, my hair loose across my shoulders. I'm getting sick of the manbun look. It was fine back when martial artists were doing it, but now, every longhair craving a straight job is trying it. Besides, I like the way Tina's gaze trails over the hair across my shoulders as I leave it free.

I flip the steaks and brush on more sauce, whistling. She sits at the little picnic table I have next to my grill as we work through the getting-to-know-you-better chitchat. Tina's like a new flower that just bloomed here; she draws a lot more attention than I think she would ever imagine.

"How's the renovation coming along?" I ask in a friendly voice. She jumps a little, and her cheeks turn colors again. I fight down a grin at the sight.

"Well, it's a whole lot of hurry up and wait, mostly. I hope the noise hasn't been bothering you." She peeks at me from behind her lashes, and this time I can't help the smile.

"Nah." I wave a hand dismissively. "I'm already up and around by the time your boys get started. You figured out yet what you want to do with the back garden?"

She shrugs, her exasperation showing a little. "Pave it over?"

I laugh. Her yard is the kind of mess that happens when someone who used to have a great space lets it go for years and years because they can't take care of it any more. Brambles, overgrown rosebushes, vines, weeds.... "I can see why you would say that," I chuckle, "But don't give up yet. You uh...still interested in working together a little?"

I have precious little free time, but I need two things right now: Tina's crush on me and her belief that I'm just a landscaper. Working every day in her back garden will give me an excuse to cultivate both.

Her eyes light up, and she takes the bait easy. "I... I'd like that. Did you have some idea of what to do with the mess back there?"

Her chest heaves distractingly with excitement, and I have to drag my eyes out of her cleavage before I answer. "Yeah, a few things. Looks like nobody's touched that garden of yours in a long time, though." I let my voice warm just a little. "It might need a lot of tender loving care."

Her expression says yes please, and I make sure to keep turned away enough that she can't see the state that just her smile has left me in. My erection throbs against the tough denim, hungry to be released and used. On her, might I add. But she's still struggling to talk gardening. "O-oh, well, then, um...you're the expert on gardens. Way more than I am."

My eyes narrow slightly with pleasure. "Yeah, you could sure say that. I'd love to come over to your place and see what I'm working with."

She smiles shyly, but with just a touch of heat in her eyes again. "Okay. After we eat, then?"

I nod, and let her off the hook by making small talk again for a while. She's already so flustered that she looks ready to fall out of her seat. Poor thing. Where has she been all her life, a convent?

The idea that she might actually be a virgin makes me want her even more. I'd love to ruin her for any man who doesn't know what he's doing in bed. I want to leave her wanting more and more. That is my idea of a great night. If, of course, I can get past her shyness.

But I've never failed at that with any woman. I can definitely break through to her no problem.

"You got something on your mind?" I ask her gently as she nibbles on bits of her steak.

She freezes for a second, then glances at me and swallows. "I guess I'm surprised you're having me over for barbecue now."

"Eh? Why is that?" I can see the tentative look on her face and know she's pushing herself to ask questions. Awkward ones. Not for me, of course; for her.

"You didn't seem...interested in talking much, before." Her fingers twiddle nervously with her silverware, and she bites her full, pink lower lip in a way that makes my mouth go dry.

"Eh, it's not because I didn't want to. I've just been really busy." I generally am. The Boss sends me on all kinds of errands, like the one I did last night. This guy needs to die, that one needs to be taught a lesson, this building needs to be torched, that one has to be protected. I've been a made man since I was seventeen, and that kind of stuff is my real day to day job. It's something I could never expect Tina to understand. "But I am interested."

I catch her gaze and hold it, and she smiles at me very shyly. But then a flicker of doubt enters her eyes. "How interested?" she asks softly.

I lift an eyebrow slightly, my smile cocky and flirtatious. "Enough to make a night of it if you've got nothing going in the morning."

Last night's hit made the news, all right, but I quickly realized when we met on the stairs that either Tina didn't watch the news too often or just didn't get a good look at Marie while I was fucking her. Either way, I was damn lucky. This time.

She hesitates, fighting down the big smile that I know wants to bloom. "Oh, I uh...thought you were seeing someone." And there it is.

I snort, cutting a big chunk of my steak and eating it before answering. "I've seen a lot of someones. I'm not serious with anyone. I wouldn't ask otherwise. I don't play those kind of games."

I want to make sure that I don't scare her off, so I try to feel her out. Once I have her nice and relaxed and into it, the games can begin. I'll get her there. I just have to learn which buttons to push.

I lean forward and catch her eye again. "What about you? You serious with anyone?"

She lets out a laugh that sounds more bitter than nervous, and I raise my eyebrows in surprise. "Never," she says simply, confirming my suspicions.

I hold her gaze a moment longer. "...Good."

6

TINA

Oh shit, did he just say that? I stare at Jimmy with my heart going a million miles an hour, flattered and shocked and still half disbelieving. I couldn't imagine this ever happening, not outside of wistful daydreams. The reality is such a pleasant shock that it is a good thing I am already sitting down.

He is watching me closely, his eyes shrewd. "You all right?" he asks me in that warm, gentle tone again.

"Yeah," I manage after a moment. "I'm okay. I'm just not used to guys like you being interested in me."

"What do you mean by 'guys like me'?" he asks, his tone staying amused even as I cringe inwardly. I was a little nervous before. Now, I feel like I'm about to do a stage solo at Carnegie Hall, and I don't play an instrument.

"I mean guys that I'm actually interested in," I force out, smiling awkwardly, my cheeks burning. I feel fifteen instead of twenty-one, full of crushes, barely understood feelings, and all sorts of euphoria and discomfort at the same time. It's so confusing to want this badly and be wanted in return.

He smiles slowly, his eyes full of heat. "Oh. Well, that explains it. You've had bad luck."

"Explains what?" I ask, so dizzy that I can barely register what he's saying to me.

He notices how flustered I am and pauses to pour me a lemonade and hand it over. I take a few grateful swallows, buying time to pull myself together. When I finally lower the glass from my lips, he speaks up. "I was trying to figure out how a catch like you could be single," he says simply.

His words race through me, waking up nerves I have never used, leaving me aching and hungry for something I'm not familiar with. I want to feel myself crushed against his sleek, hard body and held tight, until I can breathe again.

He stays where he is, and I struggle through and get over it. I take a shuddering breath. "There's an awful lot you don't know about me," I say slowly, wondering how much I should bring up, but then I realize that mentioning the nut house could scare him off; I have purposely used it to scare the wrong men off more than once.

"Now you've just got me curious." He has plowed through most of his steak already; I'm still nibbling on my first third. The flavor of the meat helps steady me. It gives me something to focus on besides the different feelings boiling around inside of me. "You feel like filling me in?"

I manage to meet his gaze. "Trade you."

He hesitates, then agrees, "Sure."

That's the first time that a little alarm bell goes off in my head about Jimmy. Just the tiniest one, set off by his hesitation as I am reminded, once again, how little I know about him, but I'm too blitzed by joy, fear, wonder, anticipation and disbelief to listen to it.

He likes me. He wants me. To Hell with everything else. I'll work it out later.

"I'm from Illinois," I start hesitantly. "Grew up in a town called Pontiac. I only ever came to New York to visit my Grandma here." It was more than a treat. This house meant safety to me when I was younger. It meant warmth; it meant comfort. It meant somewhere I was actually welcome.

"Oh, the old lady was your grandma? I heard a little about her from the neighbors, but I never talked to her much in person. Nice lady, seemed like." He devours the rest of his steak, and I have to resist the urge to offer him a chunk of mine.

"Yeah. Have you always lived in New York?" I watch his face and see that little hesitation again.

"Grew up in Yonkers. But business over there isn't anywhere as good. Here, everybody's crowded together, and any green space has to be used well. Out there, it's more like the suburbs. Only the richer people care as much." He shrugs a huge shoulder and drains most of his glass of lemonade in a few big swallows.

The flash of his throat reminds me of last night and the sight of him stretched up above that woman, every muscle taut, hips thrust hard forward and his head thrown back. The memory of that long groan of ecstasy echoes in my ears, and I almost drop my glass.

"Whoa." He catches it before it can slip from my fingers, and I stare, not realizing he could move so fast. His big, thick fingers radiate heat as they catch mine under them. "You all right?"

"Yeah, just...distracted." He wants to do that with me. He's been hitting on me. What do I do? I want it but...I've never done this. Heat and chills take turns running through my body, and I have to struggle for breath. "Sorry."

"Don't apologize." He's so close to me that I freeze, not sure what to do. He takes the glass and sets it on the table, and then lingers, his hand sliding over mine. My legs squeeze together reflexively, and I look up at him as he bends over me. "So...you never dated?"

"No. I mean, a little bit. Kid stuff." Flirting with a few of the lesser screwed-up of my fellow violent-ward inmates. Stolen kisses in the hallways. A few tentative dates the week or so after I turned eighteen. And then, nothing. "Takes a certain kind of guy to interest me. I'm picky." I say it with far more calm certainty than I actually feel.

He runs his fingertips up my arm and over my shoulder before letting me go, and leaves me sitting there shivering and craving more as he goes back to his seat. "I guess I should be flattered." But then the corner of his mouth curls. "Unless of course your bar isn't actually that high, and you've just met a lot of guys who go out of their way to go under it."

I pull out my phone and check. "Five dick pics from total strangers in the last six hours, two requests for nudes, one request for sex, one message from my stalker, and two more scammers." I look up at him meaningfully. "My bar's high. You could probably step over it easy, but it's high. Doesn't stop most guys I have met from digging into the dirt to get under it."

He lets out a laugh and refills his glass of lemonade. "I like you. So. Any family?"

Everything freezes, and I sit there blinking while I try to figure out how to handle answering. Keep it simple. "Grandma was my family."

"Oh." His smile wavers slightly. "I'm sorry."

"It's okay. I'm glad to have had her in my life." Can't say that about anyone else, really. But some people didn't even have one person to remember fondly who was tied to them by blood, so I can't complain too much. I learned that one in the nut house soon enough. "What about you?"

"Oh, well, you know, the usual. Big Italian Catholic family.

Five siblings, fifteen cousins, going on my third nephew. Most of them are local. Christmases are huge." His eyes twinkle.

"I can't imagine." A boisterous, crowded Christmas, instead of a chilly, solemn one with a gold-ornamented tree I wasn't allowed to touch? Gifts given with love instead of impersonal envelopes of money? My father even called it my "Christmas stipend" and told me I was fortunate to have it. But then again, who counts the opinion of a crazy child killer? I shake it off and turn back to my blossoming conversation with Jimmy. "How did you get into landscaping?"

"Oh, my uncle." That one he answers right away, almost eagerly. "Great guy. He raised me and my sisters along with his three kids. He wanted one of us to inherit his business, so that's what I did." He drains his glass again, and I catch his eyes sliding over me hungrily.

I don't know whether to feel powerful or frightened; I don't know whether to shrink into myself or reach out to him. It's like stage fright: the flip side of desire is this fear that somehow inexperience or my being broken will screw the whole thing up. "Guess we came from really different places then."

He shrugs, flashing another of those sexy smiles. "Well, they say opposites attract."

And just like that, he runs a callused fingertip over the back of my hand as my palm lies flat on the table. Electric sparks travel up my arm from that light, deliberate touch, and I forget every question that I was planning to ask him.

7

JIMMY

"Well, it's a jungle out here," I say cheerfully as I survey Tina's backyard. The house is even less finished than I thought; apparently only the attic suite and three of the lower rooms are fully done. She led me through the half-done kitchen to get here, and I started to understand how rough living in the middle of a renovation has been on her. But I plan to help with that—and win her heart with my yardwork as much as my cock. I put my fists on my hips as I look around.

THE OLD LADY really liked her roses. I see a dozen different colors of bloom peeking through all the tangled mess of greenery, and I can't help but smile. "You like roses like your grandma did?"

"A LITTLE. I mean, they're pretty, and they smell nice. Mostly I want to keep these ones because they remind me of Grandma."

She moves tentatively onto the overgrown mass of weeds and wildflowers the back lawn turned into.

"I'll make sure to save 'em then." I move up beside her, getting her more used to being close to me. She's skittish as a deer, and I wonder again what the hell happened to her. But this time, she doesn't move. That part, I'm glad to see.

I've dealt with girls who have been hurt by men before—lots of 'em, because there are plenty around. I don't know who these guys think they are who keep hurting women like this. I'd like to punch every last one of them in the face, but I don't mind cleaning up some of the damage they do if it gets me what I want. Besides, watching a lady bounce back from something awful and get the light back in her eyes is pretty neat. Hey, call me a romantic.

I lay my hand on Tina's shoulder and feel her tremble slightly, holding her breath. I run my fingertips over her shoulder and the side of her neck, and she lets the air out with a gasp.

"Thank you," she murmurs belatedly. We stare into the thicket for a few moments. I leave my hand where it is, and after a few shivery breaths, she lays her smooth, slim fingers on top of mine.

I feel that jolt again, all the way down to my groin, and smile to myself. I might have to take my time with this one, but not long. She's warming up to me already, even if she's tentative and shy about it. "What did this garden look like back when you were young?" I ask, getting a flash of intuition.

She lights up a little, and I feel her take a deep breath. "The rose bushes lined the two side fences, with fruit trees at the far end. She kept a lawn in the middle for her dogs and for me when I visited. There were raspberry canes climbing a trellis in the back."

"Huh. That's interesting." Dogs and high walls lined with thorny plants? I wonder what Grandma was worried about keeping out. "Big dogs?"

Tina nods. "She had a St. Bernard named Lady. The dog used to help her foster kittens for a rescue organization. Gentle as anything, but didn't look it." She doesn't move under my hand, so I slide it across her back and slip an arm around her shoulders. At once, I feel her shiver again—and every time she does, that same delicious jolt goes through me.

She points to an area of what once was a beautiful backyard. "She had a kiddie pool put up in spring and summer for that dog. Lady would just sit there soaking all afternoon." She laughs a little, high and nervous, and I suddenly realize that her head is full of things she's trying to distract herself from.

Why? Because I'm touching her? I lighten my contact a little, and she unconsciously moves closer to me. No, not that. Nice to know. But what, then?

"So, here's a question for you. What about putting the garden back the way it was, and then we'll work from there? In some ways, it will actually be easier." I turn toward her a little.

SHE LOOKS AROUND AGAIN, still trembling now and again in the circle of my arm. Then she looks up at me. "Sounds good," she murmurs. I can tell she's barely listening to what I'm saying anymore. Her mind is elsewhere, I just want to know exactly where so I can bring her back

I TAKE A RISK. It's calculated; I figure she needs to be pushed a little. Just right up to the edge of her comfort zone. My free hand cups her jawline, coaxing her head back a little more as I bend over her. Her eyes fly open in surprise and then hood almost drowsily as her hands slide up the backs of my arms.

HER MOUTH TASTES like lemonade and mint gum, and she makes a soft, little sound as I kiss her. She clings to me, trembling harder; first, she barely responds, but finally she melts into it, until finally she's kissing me back almost tenderly.

MY WHOLE BODY feels like it's burning inside suddenly. I pull her closer, my cock throbbing hard in my jeans and my mouth so hungry for hers that I don't let up for air for a long time. When I finally do, we gasp for breath as if just finishing a 400 meter dash.

She's speechless in my arms. I let her off the hook. "Wow," I breathe softly as I stare down at her. "That was really nice."

"...Uh huh," she squeaks.

I chuckle and move away just a bit, giving her a chance to catch her breath. Not to mention my need to cool down. All the blood in my body has moved into my dick, and I want to carry her up to that room she's always watching me from and fuck her brains out, but it's not time yet. Instead, I trace her delicate little lips with my fingertip and kiss her again, briefly and softly, before letting her go.

Always leave them wanting more. It's a rule. It might leave me aching too, but it would leave her curious, aroused...and less frightened.

Why is she frightened in the first place? Who the fuck hurt you, sweetheart?

"Well," I said smoothly as I stepped back, just as matter of fact as if nothing had happened. "I think I'm gonna go get my tools and get started."

. . .

"W...." she started, still looking dizzy. "What do you need from me?"

I FLASH HER A TEASING GRIN. "A six pack of good lager once I'm done and another kiss."

She blushes so hard I half expect her ankles to turn red, but then nods quickly, smiling.

ONCE BACK HOME, I set to work at once. Not on gathering tools: on gathering intelligence. This is a girl who has at least as many secrets as I do, and I want to know them all.

MY HOUSE IS DELIBERATELY nondescript on the main floor, almost like a house staged for sale. Simple but well-made furnishings, generic decor, and bland colors. It's upstairs and down in the basement, the places guests don't normally see, that get interesting.

THE HOUSE HAS two bedrooms besides the attic space, which I have turned into my computer room. It's soundproofed and heavily insulated, with air purifiers and dehumidifiers humming along with the servers and fans. One of the things I do before each job is gather intel on the targets. I guess it's the military guy in me. Before my uncle the Don took me on, I was doing a lot of the same things for the US Marines.

Tina isn't a target, but...my instincts are still going off. Something's up with that sweet little girl. Someone hurt her. And my guts twist thinking about it, making me want to find that someone and take them out. I know it's probably not possible, and depending on who it is, it might not even help her. But the impulse still tugs at me.

THE ATTIC SPACE would be stiflingly hot if it weren't for the exhaust fans pulling the warm air out, and the air conditioner pushing cool air in. Up here, I have my own high-end, liquid-cooled computer system with enough power to run a small hosting service. I tell people I'm a hardcore gamer if they ask about my appetite for tech, but I'm not. My electric bill gets pretty hefty in summer, but no one notices when everyone in the neighborhood's living on central air but me.

THE REAL NAME of the game is "intelligence gathering."

THE BIG OFFICE chair creaks under my weight as I settle into it. It's tough to find ones big and high-backed enough for me, but Uncle Ezio came through for me when he found out what I needed it for. Now he bugs me about helping him figure out all his electronics stuff, like I was his ten-year-old grandkid, but I don't mind. He may be my boss, but he's also family.

TINA CARSON OF CARSON RESTORATIONS. I find her social media accounts and her website in a few seconds. I find details on her contractor's license, her business paperwork, advertising, and some public correspondences. She has a dating site profile. It's deleted, but I know the site keeps all data for at least a year. I make a mental note to check it out.

. . .

TINA CARSON OF PONTIAC, Illinois. I try her name with the keyword "Pontiac" and find myself staring at my screen in growing horror.

MY LITTLE TINA IS FAMOUS, and not in a good way. News article after news article from almost eleven years ago pops up in my feed, and I stare at the headlines in disbelief.

"TEN YEAR OLD Murders Father With Own Handgun"
    "Killer Kid Tina Carson May Be Tried as An Adult"
    "Questions Being Asked About Carson Link to Serial Child Murder Case"
    "Mask Found at Scene Matches That Worn by Wolf's Head Killer"
    "Mother of Killer Kid Carson Calls Mask Incident That Left Husband Dead 'A Prank'"
    "Patrolman on Scene at Carson Murder Reports Bribery Attempt by Carson's Wife"
    "DNA Evidence Links Aaron Carson To Wolf's Head Murders"
    "Tina Carson Exonerated in Self Defense Killing of Child Murderer Father; Mother Seeks DA Appeal Against Own Daughter"
    "Tina Carson Admitted for Inpatient Psychiatric Treatment"
    "Carson Mother Indicted for Obstruction of Justice"
    "Carson Mother May Have Assisted Serial Killer Husband"
    "New Chapter in Tina Carson Saga as Mother Attempts to Block Inheritance"
    Holy shit. It goes on and on. My little Peeping Tina was born of monsters. One is still alive. The other, Tina killed herself, and she paid for that with her mother's hatred and imprisonment in

a psych hospital. No wonder that little hottie's a virgin—she was locked up against her will!

I DON'T HAVE time to go through all the ugly details, but that doesn't matter. She's already under my skin enough that I can feel my blood boiling. No wonder she's so skittish. No wonder she is so watchful of anything going on outside her house.

THE STRENGTH of my reaction alarms me. I barely know this girl. I know I need to manipulate her so that her observant nature doesn't turn on me. I know I want to fuck her silly—hell, I might even want to do it on the regular. I've had friends with benefits before. That could actually be workable, couldn't it?

BUT IT STILL PISSES ME OFF. She defends herself from her father, makes a mortal enemy of her mother, and ends up locked up for almost half her life because of it. It makes me want to break something. I decide to go down, grab my tools and take my anger out on the chaos of her garden. Once my anger is gone, I won't have to worry about making her nervous by just being around her. I'll cool down first.

THEN IT WILL BE time to really get down to business.

8

TINA

He kissed me.

I STAND at the window of my attic bedroom and stare down through the slanted glass at the carnage going on in my garden. Stripped to the waist save for a headscarf and heavy gloves, Jimmy's sawing, shearing, and mowing his way through almost five years of overgrowth almost as fast as it took us to talk about it. And all I can do is stare.

I HAVE the beer he wanted ready for him. Apparently, we have similar tastes, at least in that. As for the kiss…I'm watching his gleaming, dirt-streaked body labor away, cutting back the weeds and overgrowth, and my lips are tingling. I know part of it is my crush on him, but I have never gotten a kiss like that from any man before in my life.

He can have as many as he wants as far as I'm concerned.

Giddy, I have to fight to keep from hyperventilating as I watch him. He came back from next door with his burly arms full of tools and set off to work, suggesting that I get in a nap while he cleared things out. But who can sleep after a kiss like that and the promise of more?

He woke something inside of me, a wild sort of excitement that burned away almost all of my fear at once, like ice in a furnace. On one hand, it feels so much better than being afraid that I'm beaming. On the other hand, it means that when I try to go to bed, I lie there with my whole body thrumming with this unexpected emotion.

The common-sense, self-protective part of me is whispering warnings, reminding me that I don't know him that well. Reminding me that the law won't even let me get a gun to protect myself now, and if I let him into my space and my heart, he could hurt me badly enough to drive me completely crazy.

And yet....

In one way, the Doc is right. He really is. If I let myself lose my nerve all the time because of maybes, I'm never really going to live at all.

And so I watch Jimmy do battle with my overgrown garden and feel my heart bang away in my chest so hard it feels like it's going to start shaking my body. I might not know much about what happens after a kiss—not first hand—but I know that I am going to find out soon.

. . .

Jimmy seems almost angry as he rakes another mess of broken down vegetation into lawn bags. My curb is going to be lined with them before this is over. Some neighbors might complain. They're already not happy about the renovation waste dumpster taking both my parking spaces up out front.

But right now, watching him labor away, the fear I would normally feel at the idea of getting in trouble with the locals dies away quickly. It feels so good to know now that at least one of my neighbors is definitely in my corner.

And not to mention, a really, really good kisser.

I start to shake suddenly and go to lie down, staring up at the ceiling until the room stops tilting around me. I'm smiling so hard that my face aches. How long has it been since I smiled this much? Since O was seven, maybe—and in this exact same house.

I look around my attic room—my sanctum. It has a steel door on it and its own attached bathroom. It has a fire ladder I could use to climb to the ground. Its windows can't be reached from outside, and the stairs are old and noisy. I created it this way, deliberately leaving the stairs with their creaks while shoring them up from below. It isn't the most secure panic room setup I could have come up with, but it fits the space—and means that even if my stuff on lower floors might not be safe, I will sleep safely, and that's most important.

. . .

But now, I'm letting someone into that sanctum, someone who could really hurt me. But whenever he touches me, it feels so good. I want to take the risk. I want to know what it's like with someone I'm really into. Even if this never goes anywhere beyond that, even if he hurts me tomorrow and I have to jettison him out of my life, I want to know.

I stare at the heavy beam that makes up the roof-peak well over my head. The mobiles I made in art sessions over the years hang there, coated in glow in the dark paints. They are full of stars and planets, strange archaic-looking birds, and things I picked out of photos of illuminated manuscripts.

For years, I made those mobiles obsessively and hung them over my bed, like some people do a dreamcatcher. Now, dozens of them turn in the breeze from the window, and the bits of mirror glued to them send patches of light across the heavy woodwork. Will I be watching these later while he presses me into this mattress? The thought sends a happy shiver down my spine.

I must have dozed off watching the patterns of light; when I open my eyes again, the reflected light is reddening. I jump up, oddly embarrassed with myself, and hurry to the window.

I stare. The garden has been cleared. It's not quite back to the way Grandma used to have it, but it's close enough that I can imagine where the kiddie pool should be, and I can contemplate walking barefoot on the fresh-trimmed lawn. The rose bushes have been cut back a bit severely, but not enough that all the blooms are gone. The apple trees are visible again. And every last bag of cut greenery has been brought out—all but one, which Jimmy is hauling out through the alleyway on his shoulder.

I STEP BACK into my sandals, grab the beer from my tiny fridge, and hurry downstairs, thinking only of getting him his cool drink. Poor guy. Working so hard in this heat...I should let him get a shower. I'll have to fight the urge to poke my head in and watch him, but he's going to need to rinse off after all of that.

I PULL out one of the longnecks and come to meet him at the back door. He comes in panting and radiating damp heat. I offer the beer, and he immediately presses the chilled side to his temple. "Thanks, baby," he says hoarsely, his eyes tired but grateful.

"THANK YOU. I caught sight of what you did. I didn't know you were going to do everything today!" He works quickly. I wonder what that means for his sex life.

"OH, that's just the first big push," he says casually. "You've still got a lot of work to be done back there, but don't you worry about that right now anyway. It'll keep until I get some more gear in."

HE CRACKS his beer open and takes a sip, too smart to slug it down while he is overheated. "You uh...got someplace I can get cleaned up?" he asks, and I feel a catch in my chest.

"Upstairs, the attic suite. It's the only part of the house that's fully done, and it has its own bathroom." My voice comes out higher and faster than I want it to, dripping with nervousness.

"Thanks, sweetheart. I think I can manage one last set of stairs. Grab the beer, for me?" He walks past me, headed for the stairway. I stare after him for a moment, not quite sure how to react —then hastily lock the back door and hurry after him with the beer.

9
JIMMY

Seducing women is an art. You have to tailor your approach to each one of them. An alpha-female businesswoman is likely to want the polite-but-direct approach a lot more than a nervous trauma survivor, and a frustrated housewife is a lot easier to tempt than a biker chick with two boyfriends, a girlfriend, and a date list as long as your arm. Tina needs a delicate touch. I'll have her eager for something more...intense...soon enough, but for now, I'll meet her where she is.

As I climb the stairs, muscles burning from the effort after all that work and skin itching from layers of drying sweat, I know not to approach timid little Tina yet. Instead, I remind myself of what she likes to do best. She likes to watch me—preferably in as little as possible. She must have been dying to get me in the shower.

The first beer is gone in a few swallows as soon as I'm cooled down enough to keep it from giving me cramps. I'm not even up the stairs yet. Then I am, emerging into an airy, romantic space with dozens of shining mobiles hanging from the roof peak and a four-poster with mosquito netting veils sitting right beneath it. There's a small table, two chairs, a small fridge, a desk with a laptop computer, an archway that leads to the still-bright sun room, and the door to the bathroom.

"Right in there. You can, um, use one of my towels if you want." Her gaze keeps flicking over me lightly, like moth wings.

I flash a smile and stride into the antique-tiled bathroom done in shades of depression blue. I leave the door unlatched "by accident," just enough that the breeze from the small, open window inside can push it the rest of the way open. The shower stall is in full view of the door in that tiny space. All she has to do is sit somewhere where she can see it...if she doesn't walk right into the doorway altogether.

I take my time scrubbing off, turning in the spray, sighing with relief as the itch goes away and the cool water takes away the rest of that smothering feeling. She has peppermint soap and one of those scratchy loofah things. Between those and the cool water, it's more than refreshing. I feel a million times more awake by the time I rinse my hair and open my eyes.

I see her silhouette just beyond the doorway, a purple blur through the water droplets, her hands to her mouth. I stretch, letting the water sluice down my body, my cock stirring awake at her scrutiny. I watch her watch me, all the while pretending to be oblivious. When I finally turn off the water, I can hear her gasping for air as she withdraws from the doorway and steps out of sight.

I SMILE TO MYSELF. I'm clean, I'm hard, and my clothes are full of sweat, dirt and plant sap. No point in getting dressed. I take the towel she meant for me to dry off with and knot it around my hips instead, knowing it will do little to hide my erection. She likes to look, so I'll let her look.

When I come strolling out of the shower in just the towel, her jaw drops and her eyes widen, and I almost burst out laughing. Hi there! "Can't put those clothes on, they're messed up. Do you have a working washer?"

"B...BASEMENT," she mumbles, gaze glued to my crotch, and I chuckle and lift an eyebrow at her.

"MIND if I clean them up later? I'm really in no hurry to get dressed again. Unless it bothers you." I keep my tone so casual, it almost sounds lazy, and see her swallow a thought down.

"BOTHER ME?" she murmurs, and then laughs and shakes her head. "Not really. The truth is...I like to look." She chews her lip nervously and admits, "All I've ever been able to do before is look. So I like it."

"SHY GIRL." I walk toward her, the tented towel leading the way. I see her keep trying not to stare and failing, and it just amuses me more. "Well...feel free to look all you want."

· · ·

SHE LICKS HER LIPS, her tiny pink tongue tip lapping at their full curves, and her gaze slides over me like a hand. My loins tighten further; it almost hurts. But as I stand there, and she walks around me, moving close at times but not touching, I can sense the heat starting to rise in her as well. The shiver in her breath. Her dilated eyes.

I SMILE AT HER, reassuring, inviting. By the time this is done, she'll be hooked enough to keep any secret I feel like telling her. I bet everything on it, and I never lose.

SHE COMES AROUND in front of me again, and I see she has her hand raised, but is still keeping it to herself. She steps toward me just a little, and I close the distance a little more. She looks up at me, her eyes searching my face. I don't know why she's hesitating, but I discipline myself. Patience is going to win me this one, and I know it will be worth it in the end.

"YOU CAN TOUCH, TOO," I urge her gently. She bites her lip briefly again, and then reaches out, laying her hand on the side of my neck.

I TILT my head like a tiger being petted as her fingers wander through the wet waves of my hair, then over my shoulder. Her breath is starting to come in little sips, and her warm, dry fingers slide over my dampness-cooled skin in a way that leaves tingling trails in their wake. I've never been this eager to have a woman touch me, and I've never fought this hard to keep things at her pace.

She brushes her fingertips down my chest and belly, and then shies away at the edge of the towel. We aren't quite there yet, but she's getting braver. Soon, her warm palms slide up my back as she steps into my arms.

This time, when I kiss her, she kisses me back, and that single touch of boldness sets me on fire inside. My cock throbs insistently, trapped against my belly through the terrycloth as she pushes against me. "Holy shit, sweetheart," I groan in her ear as the kiss breaks. "You've really got my number." And I kiss her again, fiercely, letting my passion for her sink in. When it does, she starts trembling again.

Her fingers shy toward my ass and then caress it through the towel. I smile against her lips and hold her one-armed for a moment while I unknot the towel between us. It slips to the floor, and my cock springs free, rubbing against the slightly rough gauze of her dress.

She freezes, blinking in shock as her hands land on the bare skin of my ass, and for a moment, I think I must have gone too far. But then she looks up at me, and her hands start to caress and knead, her nails brushing the skin of my ass, and then around to my hips and over my belly. And just when I think I can't get any harder, her small, gentle hand settles on my cock.

I let out a sharp little shout as the jolt goes through me, so hard that my cock trembles and weeps a tear of precum. Her fingers smooth it into my skin as she explores my head and shaft with a strange intensity, as if memorizing every inch of me by touch. "Ah...sweetheart...mm. That's good."

My balls are so tight to my body that I can feel it. Every inch her fingers slide over me makes the tension mount inside of me just a little bit more. When she finally circles my cock with her hands and milks it gently, I groan and thrust my hips.

I finally have to stop her, gently taking her hands in mine. "Okay, baby. I need a break, or I'm going to cum all over that pretty dress of yours." I lift an eyebrow and tilt my head. "In fact, I'm probably going to mess it up either way. Maybe you'd like to take it off?"

She stares at me for a moment...and then nods, the tiniest smile on her face. I watch her start to unfasten the long row of buttons that runs down the front of the dress, and my mouth goes dry. Slowly, she pulls the fabric off her shoulders, her eyes still shy behind her lashes.

The black satin bra underneath is a nice surprise. No lace, smooth and gleaming, accentuating her pale skin. I hold still, just as she did, content to watch for now, but my body is so hungry for hers that it hurts.

10

TINA

His skin is warm and smooth, and he shudders under my hands, his breath catching as I finally get to touch him the way I have dreamed of doing. He responds so much to every little caress, filling me with a completely foreign sense of power. I realize slowly that despite his ability to overpower me physically, I am the one in control right now. He has given me that.

I don't know how he knows that I need so much care. Maybe his instincts are just this good. Or maybe he's this gentle with every woman. Though from what I saw last night, that doesn't seem to be the case. I finally get it through my head to stop mulling on it so much and enjoy it instead.

When I touch his cock, I know at once that all my careful explorations are really turning him on. He trembles; he moans; his shaft throbs under my hand as I caress his silky skin. It's big, thick, enough that I wonder how it could fit inside of me without hurting. Guess I'll find out, I think a little nervously. I want it, but I fear it a little as well.

This time when we kiss, I don't freeze up. This time, when the kiss ends, he asks me to take the dress off. And I do. Slowly, hesitantly, but my fingers do the work without fumbling, and soon I slip the garment off over my shoulders. Thank God I wore a pretty bra today, I think nervously as he stares at me.

My knees are starting to feel weak, so I take his hand and lead him over to the bed. It's huge; I like to stretch out, especially in the heat. Now, I settle onto it and look up at him as he walks toward me, his cock trembling slightly in the air between us.

He walks up, bends over me, and captures my mouth again; this time, I fall back onto the bed, and he clambers up to crouch atop me. His cock throbs against my belly as he covers my face and neck with slow kisses, the hand not bracing him above me starting to move over my skin.

His hand is huge and callused, his touch firm without being rough. He runs it up and down my side, then cups my hip and starts caressing it through my boy shorts. Electric shocks of pleasure run from my hip and up and down the length of my belly, gathering in my untouched clit, which almost aches now for some kind of contact. I moan softly as his tongue tip runs down my throat into its hollow, then moves lower, dipping into my cleavage.

Now and again as he caresses me, I start to get scared. I breathe deep then and try to focus on what he's doing to me, not on the shyness or the apprehension. It gets easier as I start to lose myself in sensation, another layer of ice melting away from our heat.

He kisses me through and around the cloth of my bra, running his fingers under it in back and teasing them against my skin. His mouth grows more and more aggressive, nipping and nibbling through the satin until my nipples are so hard they ache a little.

I want more. I want his mouth on my skin. I whimper and arch, struggling to put words together, then I start reaching back to unfasten the bra myself.

He moves up, and his mouth comes down on mine roughly again, and at the same moment I feel his deft fingers unhook the catch. The cups loosen; I eagerly shrug out of the straps and toss the bra to the floor.

He feels the slide of my breasts against his chest and groans into my mouth, then draws back to look at me. I stare back at him shyly and see the fascinated delight on his face as he gazes at the breasts I have shown exactly no man before no matter how much they begged. The look sends a warm feeling all through me that only makes the ache in my cunt worse.

He cups one of my breasts reverently, and then starts to kiss it, first on the ordinary skin covering most of it, then starting to spiral inward toward the more sensitive parts. Each kiss feels good, but as he draws closer and closer to my nipple, I start shivering again, and my back arches in a silent plea.

Then, his mouth closes on my nipple and he suckles long and easy. My body tightens as the unfamiliar pleasure rolls through me. The ache in my cunt intensifies, starting to throb in time with his suckling. I can't speak; the only thing coming out of me now is wordless croons.

He moves to my other nipple and suckles it, tweaking and rubbing the first with his fingertips. I squirm, my mind whiting out with completely unfamiliar sensations. My hips roll and shimmy against him by themselves. I hear my own voice begging for more, and I know I can't control it, not even for a moment.

My cunt is tightening like a fist inside of me, and my clit aches. My back arches slowly as I let out a pleading whimper. Then his hand slides down my belly and cups my mound through my panties. He kneads it gently; I gasp desperately, the sensation rolling through my hips and making them rock and shiver.

It's happening. He's doing it. He's really going to do it.

I lift my hips again and feel him slide my panties off. I don't even think to protest. Why would I?

His fingers start exploring my cunt, very gently and slowly, giving me time to get used to it. He rubs the outside, then slides his fingertip into me and runs it up and down my slit lazily as he keeps pleasuring my breasts. I can sense his eyes on my face as he works, but my vision is dim and blurry, and I finally just close my eyes.

I'm already getting impatient. I crave something...and as his finger starts caressing around and above my clit, it feels so good. Somehow, it only makes that craving worse.

He's panting, and I feel the head of his cock slide over my skin as he backs off and pulls me by the hips to the edge of the bed. He goes back to caressing me—and as I start to moan uncontrollably, he picks up the pace.

So good...everything in me wants to scream out how amazing it feels. Instead, I'm cooing and sobbing and rolling my hips against his hand as something inside me winds tighter and tighter, like a spring about to snap back hard.

He slows down just a touch and smiles down at me as I open my eyes. "Are you ready for it, baby?" he purrs, and I feel the push of something hot and slick against my lower lips.

It's time. I've reached the point where I crave him so much that there's no room for fear at all any more. I draw a deep breath and nod.

He starts stroking me fast again, leaving me pushing hard against him as he starts sliding into me. His girth stretches me almost painfully; his eyes widen as his cock pushes in to fill me, and then close as he groans aloud.

He holds me against him with one arm while the other hand works its magic between my thighs. I close my eyes, feeling his cock trembling slightly as he holds still, not thrusting yet. His finger keeps stroking and stroking, and every touch drives me even crazier. My mind seems to center on my clit and collapse inward towards it, until sensation is all I have room for in my head.

My muscles clench around his cock, tighter and tighter as it feels better and better, and then the pleasure gets so intense that I'm screaming.

My back arches hard, and my cunt suddenly contracts around his shaft, milking it rhythmically as a torrent of sensation runs through my nerves. Pleasure explodes through me again and again as I grind against him with all my strength.

He groans hard at my writhing and starts to thrust, his belly slapping against mine as he keeps stroking me. I clutch him to me, arching against him as he starts to pound into me. His eyes are closed; his lips are parted, and long, low shouts burst out of him with every movement of his hips. The wave of relaxation that was settling over me gives way to fresh sensation; every thrust of his cock sends a fresh jolt through my nerves.

I hang on for dear life as his powerful body moves against mine, my body starting to tighten and tremble again. He heaves against me on sheer instinct now, animal groans and growls pushing out of his lips as his fierce movements creak the bed. I squeal, heels digging against his hips, nails in his back, my hips rolling hard as my nerves ramp up toward ecstasy again. Then it hits, and I sob for joy.

He thrusts faster and faster, the strain on his face even more beautiful and sexy when close up, and I lift my hips to meet him as he moves. His lips part again, and his guttural cries nearly put me over the edge again just by themselves.

His muscles lock—and he roars with pleasure as he grinds his hips against me. I feel his cock jolt inside of me as he thrusts a few more times, and then shudders to a stop. He collapses over me with a satisfied sigh, barely remembering to catch himself.

It's done. I'm sure some of my muscles will be sore in the

morning, but it didn't hurt...and now, I know. I hold Jimmy as his body relaxes over me, his head on my shoulder and his breath going slow and steady.

I know what an orgasm feels like now; it's so intense that it almost scares me. But I want more of it. I want it with him, again and again. Only him.

11

JIMMY

I cum harder than I ever have in my life, and for a while afterward all I can do is just lay there, legs half off the bed, catching my breath. The smell of her sweat and sex fills my nostrils, and I relax in her arms, so deeply that I almost fall asleep.

Except of course that she's half my size, and tough little thing or not, we need to change positions. I slide out of her reluctantly and stand, my legs surprisingly wobbly. She lies there drowsily, hair tangled across the bedspread and her soft, pale breasts rising and falling with her breath. No blood and no sign of pain. That's how you do it, I think proudly before gathering her against my chest and picking her up.

She makes a soft, interrogative sound, and I smile and nuzzle her hair before pulling aside the covers and nestling her into the bed. I should leave her to sleep. I should. I have a job tonight, and I shouldn't get too attached. This can't be a romance. I'm a killer.

Of course, so is she, but in her case, it was about as justifiable as a homicide gets. I can't say that about anything I do. I won't end up raped and strangled in an alley somewhere if I don't kill my target. Uncle Ezio wouldn't be happy with me, and there would be consequences, but that's not exactly the same.

I stare down at her for a moment, then find myself sliding in next to her and wrapping around her from behind. She's so soft and warm in my arms, and I'm tired from hard work and good screwing. I'll just lie here a while....

Uncle Ezio looks down at me sadly as I crouch over the toilet. I'm fourteen, my hands smell of gunsmoke, and my stomach keeps heaving long after I have anything left to bring up.

I made my first kill today.

The guy was going to shoot Uncle Ezio and I as we were coming out the back of the theater. Matinees have been our special thing to do together since he took me in. He's watched so many cheesy kids' shows with me that he's memorized some of them, but he never complains. After a while, I've realized that he wanted to be a dad more than my real dad ever had. I was just the lucky kid he took care of. I was happy that day.

And then suddenly, in broad daylight no less, some hitter from a rival family had stepped out from behind a dumpster and pointed his gun at us.

Ezio went for his gun while pushing me behind him, and the guy shot him in the shoulder. It spun him around, and his gun dropped at my feet. I screamed, scooped it up, and fired wildly at the man.

Now the mob doc has patched Ezio's shoulder up, and our boys have cleaned up the mess. But all I can do is gag and choke and puke and cry like a little kid with the stomach flu.

I'm cleaning myself up, still shaking, when I feel my uncle's leathery hand settle on my shoulder. "It's all right, kid," he says in his thick accent. I look up, and his eyes are kind and without pity or judgment. "I threw up for three days when I killed my first guy."

"You did?" I'm shocked. Uncle Ezio doesn't seem to be afraid of anything.

He looks at me solemnly. "Yeah. I did. And that was a straight up job. You, you defended us. You saved both our lives, kid. You did good. But it's still gonna hurt because you've got a heart.

"Even when that guy is a total scumbag, his wife probably isn't. His kids probably aren't. You kill somebody, you take responsibility for the suffering of everyone who loves the guy. Even knowing that it has to be done, even going through with it, you're gonna feel at least a little sick because deep down, you know that it's wrong. We don't kill because it's right, kid. We kill because somebody has to die. If you're gonna be a hitter for me, you gotta know that."

My eyes open onto the dim light of sundown and a thousand orange sparks from the mirrored mobiles hanging overhead. A soft, warm weight against my side whimpers softly. I turn my head and see Tina nestled in the crook of my arm, trembling in the grip of a bad dream.

"Wake up, sweetheart." I lean over and whisper in her ear. She mumbles something and stirs. "That's it. Just a dream. That's all. It'll be okay."

I kiss her ear, and she relaxes against me with a sigh. Then, I go back to staring at the ceiling. I have some time. I can stay, if I want. The hit happens late; this one, a crooked DA's assistant, will get a few drops of something in his nightcap, and the embolism he's been fighting for two years will give. I could even use her as an alibi by fucking her to sleep again and then leading her to think I never left.

That's actually a good idea. And it gives me a good excuse to stay. Except....

I stroke her red hair back from her face and kiss her behind her ear. Yeah. I could really get used to this.

I think that more than once in the next few hours. We share

a pizza, and I have her for dessert, my tongue lashing against her sweet little clit until she can't scream anymore and finally goes limp. I cum in her twice, and we finish the beer before we curl up to sleep for a while. Or she does.

When she falls asleep, I pull the tiny syringe out of my leather bracer and bend over her. Hold still, sweetheart, you won't even wake up with a headache after this. But even though I know it won't do anything but make her sleep deeper, I stop suddenly.

What am I doing? This is sick.

It's worse than sick. It's safe to assume that she's been forced onto some psych med. What if there's a drug interaction? What if I hurt her?

I don't want to hurt her. I don't even want to disappoint her. She's had enough of that!

I sit there hesitating, confused. My head is whirling. I lower the needle toward her vein again, thinking of how important it is to complete this job and how it could be dangerous as well if she woke up at the wrong moment. But....

What the hell am I doing, drugging my girlfriend? Is that what I've come to? Wait a minute? Girlfriend? I must be losing it.

Time is getting short. I have to leave. I dress quickly in my dirty clothes just to get across the street, change into my work gear and a fresh pair of gloves, and get on the road.

I'm caught in traffic in Midtown when I get a text from my uncle.

Kid. Watch out. Tonight's guest is friends with Di Lorenzo.

"Fuck." The Di Lorenzo brothers are holdouts from the last family that held the Five Boroughs. They refuse to swear to my uncle and instead have tried to build their own little rival empire. It's more than a little ridiculous, given that they have about ten guys and we have three hundred, but I do have to give them credit for balls.

Caution, too. The problem in this case is that every time the guys manage to buy a politician, they end up guarding him with their lives. Assistant DA David Grace is their biggest asset. No doubt he'll be guarded.

I quickly text a reply. Advice?

There's a long pause before he answers, and I move up some in the stop-and-go traffic. Finally, he texts I'll have some of the guys give them something to do while you do your job.

I feel a creeping surge of doubt and want to ask him to send someone else. But then I just shake my head at myself. Man up. Of course you'd rather be back in bed with Tina. Who wouldn't? But the job was in my life before Tina, and I have to do it.

Grace's mansion, where he lives on his own save for a small army of servants, sits on half an acre in the middle of the most expensive real estate in America. I have already cracked his camera and alarm codes; I just have to get in and out unseen. I don't know how Uncle Ezio is planning to lead the others away from me, but I am grateful that he is trying something.

Unfortunately, it looks like he hasn't put his plan in motion yet, and I can see four guys prowling around the property that weren't there when I scouted it. I drive by at a normal pace, park two blocks past the grounds entrance, and get over the electrified fence with the help of a leather jacket and my vaulting skills.

I watch from the shadows, poison in my pocket, while I wait for Ezio's distraction. I don't know what I should be expecting. A car full of hitters? Someone showing up with tranquilizer darts? You never really know with my uncle.

Then it happens: there is a muffled boom, and suddenly car alarms go off down the street. I look from behind a bush and smirk. There's a black Cadillac on fire down the street, its own alarm shrilling—and suddenly all four men are running out the gate yelling and pulling at their hair. My car, my car.

Snickering, I make my way inside, texting Ezio on the burner phone. I'm in.

It takes a little risky sneaking around, but I finally make my way to the study and look in to see Grace sipping his nightly brandy in a wing-back chair. He's barely touched it yet; I'm still on time. OK he is in his study.

A second later, deep in the house, a phone starts ringing. Grace sighs and gets up, shuffling out of the room while I hide around the corner and head off down the hall toward the sound. I look around, then slip into the room and withdraw a dropper bottle from the inside of my hoodie. I put ten flavorless drops into his drink, tuck the bottle back into my pocket, and see myself out. Once I get back over the fence, I text Ezio briefly. Done.

I put on my safety light and start jogging toward my car, pretending to be out for a late-night run. It takes me right past the now-smoking car—and three very angry guys from the Di Lorenzos, currently yelling Italian into their phones as they bitch about their blown-up ride. Heh. Sorry boys. But you know what they say. All's fair in love and gang war.

One of them frowns suspiciously as I jog past with my head-phones in and no music playing. I feel his eyes follow me down the street, but he says nothing. I relax after a minute and finally reach my car, getting in. Things are fine. What are the odds that any of them are going to want to tail me back to Brooklyn just because of a funny feeling?

12

TINA

I wake up screaming from my usual nightmare and this time, there's no Jimmy there to comfort me. Confused and then hurt, I roll over and look around. He's gone; his clothes are gone. Heart sinking, I move to the window and see that all the lights in his house are out.

It shouldn't bother me. We both wanted sex. We didn't say anything about his staying the night. We didn't say anything about any kind of ongoing relationship. We really didn't say anything at all. But the ache I feel inside of me as I shower off just won't go away.

He's my first, and I'm trying to keep my head on straight about it. But it's not easy. In fact, I feel like I'm going to start crying as I get dressed. I know I can't sleep again tonight. My emotions are out of line; I have no business having any real expectations of him besides things like treating me right in bed and not stealing my stuff. And he's already done so much.

I drag me and my aching heart downstairs, planning to look at my garden in the moonlight. That is real, just as what Jimmy did to my body is real. I can see my grandmother's roses and apple trees again. It's not some sign that Jimmy was just using me that he didn't choose to stay the night.

But I wish he had.

I mope around for a while, going upstairs to check social media on my laptop. This time, instead of just deleting dick pics and reporting their senders, I go off. You're disgusting, I tell them in a copy and pasted message.

I run a business web site, and because idiots like you can't control your libidos, I have to deal with sexual harassment all day. I will be reporting you and your small, ugly dick to IG staff. Bye.

It's three in the morning, and I still get replies. Mostly whining.

I thought u would like it :(

I just need help getting off babe send nudes

You slut you know you like this dick

I shake my head, sigh, block, report, and screen shot all three of them—and am finishing up when I hear a car drive up outside.

I jump up and run to the street side window—and see Jimmy's nondescript blue sedan pulling up in front of his brownstone. My heart leaps. He gets out yawning, looks up at my window, and smiles. I wave to him excitedly, but I don't think he sees me. Instead, he pulls out a six pack of beer and a bag from one of the only late-night groceries around, shuts his door, and starts walking up my steps.

He was just out for food and beer! He planned to come back all along! Beaming, I run down the stairs in my nightgown, headed for the front door to let him in.

For some reason, he doesn't knock or come to the door. Confused, I move forward and look out the nearest window. He's stopped halfway up the stairs. Did he forget something?

I open the door for him, smiling widely. "Jimmy! Hey, I thought you had left."

He looks back at me quickly, startled, and I see his face is pale and his eyes full of warning. "Baby, get back inside—" he starts.

"Hey, asshole." The voice shouts from down on the sidewalk behind him, and he turns quickly, dropping his groceries. The beer shatters, sending foam and shards of glass down the steps. I can't see what's going on, but he suddenly shoves me back through the door hard enough to send me sliding on my butt into the next room. A loud noise sounds at the same time, but I'm so shocked I barely hear it.

I let out a startled squeak, sore butt tingling, and start to yell at him when I see two bullet holes in the door right where I was standing. Jimmy is mid-spin, reaching under his jacket. I see a bullet hole in the hem. His hand draws back and pulls out an enormous black pistol with a strange cylinder fastened to the end of it.

What in the world...?

I clap both hands over my mouth and watch as he fires twice at whoever is at the bottom of the stairs. The gun lets out low thumps instead of loud reports; I hear a gurgling cry and then a thud.

Jimmy stands there panting and then lowers the gun. He turns to me—and past him I see a crumpled figure on the ground, hand still loosely gripping a smaller pistol.

Oh God, I think as my guts turn to ice water. He just killed someone right in front of me who was trying to kill him. Why was someone trying to kill him? Why does Jimmy have a huge, silenced gun tucked under his jacket?

"J...Jimmy?" I whisper, breathless with disbelief.

His face falls, and he shakes his head, putting the gun away.

He looks back at his ruined groceries, then sighs and steps forward to offer a hand.

I shrink back away from him. Who is he? What the hell did he just do?

He winces, and takes a step back. "Tina...baby...."

"You just killed somebody right in front of me! And you were ready for it!" My voice is a thin whisper, but from his tight expression, I can tell he can hear me. "Who are you? What are you?"

"Can we talk about this inside?" he says in an almost pleading tone, catching me off guard. I realize suddenly that the more we talk outside, the more likely the neighbors will notice. The one unsilenced gunshot could be chalked off to a car backfiring, but ongoing drama afterward?

I stare at him as I get up, wanting more than anything to slam the door in his face—or maybe throw myself at his feet and beg him to tell me that this was all some kind of bizarre, entirely fake prank. Tears roll down my cheeks, which makes him wince again.

"Can I trust you?" I whisper. He goes very quiet as if he doesn't know the answer himself. Then, he reaches for me again.

I shake my head. "No. Please. Go away. Please just leave me alone!"

I slam the door in his face and lock it, run for the stairs, lock the steel door at its top behind me, and throw myself on my bed sobbing.

13

JIMMY

The next three days are some of the most hellish in my life. Not just because Ezio had to help me do an emergency cleanup right in front of my house. Not just because the Di Lorenzos were on the warpath now that Grace was dead. But because my little Peeping Tina is gone. She's gone without being gone.

She's locked up in her house. Now and again, one of her guys brings groceries over. The trash gets taken out, and at night, I see lights over there, but she hasn't left. Not once.

I did this. I fucked up. I should have left her alone. Now, she's gone, and hurt, and worst of all of it is that she walked away with my heart in her fucking pocket. I can't stop thinking about her.

I managed to find the right girl for me and lose her, all in the span of one single goddamn night.

I don't know what to do. This is the one thing I can't go to my uncle about. She knows too much, and I know the rules. He might send me to kill her. I can't risk that, so I don't tell him.

The cleaners got the body out of there before anyone noticed it, along with the second car that I had not noticed driving because—hooray for irony—I was busy thinking of Tina. I still half expected the police to show up at my door after the first day, but Tina didn't call them.

The days crawled. I worked, and slept, and watched Tina's house for signs of life. And every damn day that went by, the hurt and the sick feeling in my stomach got worse.

But life goes on, even when you don't want it to. I have to keep in shape, I have to keep alert for any further trouble, and I have to figure out what excuse I could possibly give Ezio if Tina decides to blab about what she has seen.

I go out on the fourth morning since Tina slammed the door in my face, I strip down, and go through my exercises as usual. Now and again, I glance up at the windows of the sun room, hoping that I will see a small, curvy shape hiding behind the thin gauze curtains, but I don't.

I double my normal routine, pushing myself well beyond pain, punishing my body for my crimes. Crimes against Tina mainly, whom I wish every hour of every day that things had gone differently with. Against myself, for making so many mistakes, even if my heart was in the right place. And against that punk who shattered my chance at something good with a burst of bullets.

I'm bathed in sweat by the time I'm done; my limbs are slack with exhaustion, and I'm ready for a shower. I look up again, just in case—and see Tina standing there, in that same purple dress.

She hasn't been sleeping. I can tell that from where I'm standing. Her eyes are sunken, her skin is pale, and as she lays her slim hand against the glass longingly, I turn and look up at her openly, wishing I could cross the distance between us.

She hesitates...but then steps back into the darkness, out of sight. My heart sinks, and I sigh. I want her back badly. I want my chance back. But will she ever allow it?

Four days become five, and five become six. I drink too

much. I work out in the mornings. She watches. Then she goes back inside and doesn't call me or knock on my door.

But she still hasn't called the police.

I can't touch another woman while I'm waiting for her. I come to realize it as I look up at her staring down at me on the eighth morning. I was bringing home women almost every night for a month before this, but now I don't even go down to the club. There's just no point. I'll only be thinking of Tina anyway.

I'm drinking hard on the eighth night. I don't even care anymore. Bourbon and beer, too much of both. I get it in my head to visit her.

The night air slaps my face coolly as I step out onto my porch. I know right away that the booze is giving me stupid ideas, but I keep walking anyway. Down the stairs. Down the sidewalk. Up her stairs. Up to her door.

Don't do this, I tell myself. You're drunk. You will make a fool of yourself.

Except I'm already a fool. And I'm here recognizing that and begging for her mercy, which she will need to have a lot of once she has the whole truth.

I knock on the door and brace myself. After over a minute, she finally comes up to the other side.

For a moment, I expect her to see me through the peephole and immediately hurry away, refusing me again. The possibility twists a knife in my gut. I square my shoulders, taking a deep breath, and wait.

Then, the door unlocks. My eyes widen, and when she finally opens the door and looks up at me, I have no idea what to say.

She seems to understand. Or maybe she's having trouble with words herself. Whichever it is, after a moment, she steps back to let me in.

Not one to question my good luck, I step in after her, and close the door behind us.

14

TINA

"I'm not supposed to tell you about my job," he says slowly as we sit in my now-finished living room. The new cream leather couch under him creaks softly as he sits across from me. I curl into the matching recliner and watch him quietly for now. "In fact, if I did it could get us both killed."

"Why? No one would believe me even if I told the police, which I wasn't going to do anyway." My voice comes out a sigh.

The last week has been a nightmare. I have stopped dreaming of the night my father died, and instead, I dream of Jimmy. The taste of his kiss. The way it felt to be held by him. The incredible, explosive pleasure I had felt in that moment as he brought me to my first climax. I wanted him back. I didn't dare call him. All I could do for a week was dream, and cry, and putter away a little at projects by myself.

"You don't think they would believe you?" That's a surprise...and then, it isn't.

"When I was ten, I killed my dad with a pistol like yours. He had gone off the rails and was killing local kids while dressed in a wolf mask. I was his next victim, but I had started keeping the gun in my room since I found out where they hid it. I didn't know it was him behind the mask, but when he came for me, I shot him." I swallow down the fear tightening my throat and look at him firmly.

"They called me a 'killer kid' and wanted to try me as an adult. The cops and the justice system, my mother...they all put me through hell. I've never called the police for anything after that. I don't trust them. If I could have a gun, I would just get one and protect myself that way."

"I can get you a gun," he volunteers quickly. I know he's trying to make things right, but I wince anyway. His face falls slightly. "Sorry."

"I know you're not law enforcement." I chew my lip as I look at him. "Even spooks don't have shootouts with mysterious men in the middle of a New York neighborhood."

"No," he admits. "They don't. So...you don't ever call cops?"

"Cops have never made anything better in my life." I can't keep the bitterness out of my voice, and he nods in sympathy.

"Then...who do you go to for justice? If not the system?" He keeps gazing at me longingly, and it makes my knees squeeze together.

"I don't have anyone I can go to. I'm an outsider. They made sure of that." I struggle with words, trying to explain. Trying to explain why he doesn't need to fear me or any ability that I have to expose him. But do I need to fear him?

"I could...fix that too." Even though he's clearly had too much to drink, I can still sense his hesitation. "If you want it."

I know he's talking about some mob boss somewhere, the same sort that runs almost every city on the East Coast. "I spent a week thinking about this. About you. About what I've been through. And yeah, maybe it's best you don't give me details about your job. I don't want you getting in trouble. But...."

I look back at him, thoughtful, tired, and craving his touch again with every fiber of my being. He stares back at me, licking his lips, that puppy-dog longing in his dark eyes again. "I miss you."

"I miss you too, baby. I miss you like air. Is there any fucking chance at all for me or should I be packing up and moving out of the neighborhood? I can't look up at your window every morning and not want you."

Those eyes. My vision blurs with tears, and I smile through them. "Everyone thought I was a monster. A lot of them still do. My mother hates me. Keeps saying my dad was innocent and I killed him for no reason. So I...can't just...think you're a monster...without giving you a chance to explain."

He goes quiet and then looks back up at me. "My uncle Ezio's not in landscaping. I work for him. It's probably better not to ask too many questions even if you keep secrets well. You could be...you know...dragged into things. Which is why I didn't go near you for a long time." He flashes a rueful grin. "Not that I didn't want to. I've been watching you for months."

He's making me blush again. He sees it, and hope rises in his eyes.

"Look," he says slowly. "I'm drunk, and I'm an asshole, and I do things wrong. All I know is, when I was with you, none of those things happened. I was just happy being with you, that's all. I wanted to see where that went. I wanted...I still want it."

He kills people for a living. Probably for some mob boss. I would never quite know where he is or what he is up to when it comes to his job. But that's for both our protection. And if he's such a monster...why do I feel safe around him? Why is he kind to me?

"You make me feel things I've never felt," I say breathlessly. "I can't just ignore that."

He scoops me into his arms and kisses me, putting everything into it, so that I'm dizzy by the end. There's a plea in that kiss and a promise.

He's drunk, but it only makes him more honest and more vulnerable. I know he's telling the truth. And maybe I really am crazy, but after a lifetime of everything reversed—the monster father, the hateful mother, the lawmen who tried to arrest a child, and the press that chose spectacle over truth—maybe one last contradiction is exactly what I need.

He pushed me out of the way of two bullets, and he shot the man who would have killed us both. Can a killer be noble? If a father can be a monster, then why not?

When the kiss breaks, I feel a weight lift from me, the sudden freedom leaving me almost giddy. I give him a tiny smile. "There's just one condition."

His eyebrows raise. "What is that?"

"No more bringing your work home with you. Okay, honey?" There's a warning behind those words, but I smile with good humor, and after a moment, he chuckles.

"I promise," he says, before leaning down to kiss me again.

The End.

SIGN UP TO RECEIVE FREE BOOKS

Sign Up to Receive Free E-Books and Audiobook Codes.

Would you like to read **The Unexpected Nanny, Dirty Little Virgin** and **other romance books** for **free**?

You can sign up to receive these free e-books and audiobooks by typing this link into your browser:

https://www.steamyromance.info/free-books-and-audiobooks-hot-and-steamy/

Or this one:

https://www.steamyromance.info/the-unexpected-nanny-free/

PREVIEW OF THE PROMISE OF LOVE
A BILLIONAIRE ROMANCE

By Scarlett King

Blurb

Ben Donovan owns a large corporation, and he is also known as a philanthropist for all his good deeds around the world. A scandal breaks out when his company is associated with an oil leak in the ocean. His team is on damage control, and they have to fix his reputation. His right-hand man suggests that he go to Africa to help build a school—it's a good PR move.

When he arrives in Africa, Ben comes across do-gooder Katie Bennett. The two have an instant connection, but when Katie finds out how Ben's been trying to cover up the oil leak back home, she questions everything she's learned about him. He tries to explain himself, but she shuts him down and ends up leaving Africa. Ben knows they have something special, but when he tries to win her back, he just might be too late.

I knew he was in the room before I entered it.
His gaze was that intense.
I tried to ignore it, but there he was.
He consumed my every thought.
I knew what I wanted though and I would not be played.
Come to me Ben, claim me as your own.
I needed him…
Ben Henricks knew how to touch me; I was powerless under his touch.
Can I risk everything, my heart for him?

His hands did pleasing things to my body.
I needed his touch.
My first orgasm came from his rough touch.
I couldn't help but moan when he touched me.
I ached for him, his touch, his mouth.
It broke me when I left him.
He was all I ever thought about.
Could I live without him? I wasn't sure…
When he touched me, I couldn't say no.

CHAPTER ONE

Ben

I sat at the head of the boardroom table, disgusted as I glanced around the room. I couldn't believe what had happened to my own company in such a short amount of time. What was the matter with the people I employed? How could such a disaster go unnoticed until it practically blew up in our faces—and in the news of all places? It was enough to make me blow my top, and I did just that.

"Shut up, all of you! I'm sick of listening to this blathering mess. Why don't you tell me who's responsible for this disaster!"

All heads turned to me in alarm. They were terrified of me, and they had every reason to be. I may be a young billionaire, but I ran a tight ship and I wasn't about to have anyone employed by me running around creating scandals at my company. I got to the top for a reason; I was damn smart.

There was silence all around the room. I looked at each and every one of my advisors and saw their fear reflected back to me.

A bunch of cowards, that's all they were. My company's reputation was being dragged through the mud, and they had nothing to say about the matter.

"I'm waiting."

They all stared at me in awe. They knew darn well that I wasn't the kind of boss that anyone messed with, and I knew they were all wondering if they would be fired that day. I might have to just let them all go and start with a fresh team the next day; I was that fed up with them. I needed the best people on my team, and they had fallen short lately. I wasn't sure how I was going to handle the situation, but I had to figure out a way to get my company out of the mess it was in before it was destroyed forever.

The company had recently been charged with criminal and —my god—federal charges for dumping industrial waste into the Arctic Ocean. The Arctic Ocean! Just thinking about that mess brought a rage in me that was barely contained. What was worse was that I had no idea these practices were going on behind my back. That was some moron's solution to getting rid of company waste: to pollute an ocean instead. It sickened me just thinking about it. I had to admit I was angrier at myself than at anyone else. I wasn't sure how something so massive could possibly get past me. How had I not known what was going on behind the scenes? Maybe I had been playing a little too much in life and not spending enough time getting dirty at my own company. That had to be it, right? I just wasn't paying attention, and now the company—*my* company—was paying the price.

I looked around the room again, trying to summon up some clarity on the whole situation. Could that be found?

"Imagine my surprise, ladies and gentlemen, when I return from a lovely vacation only to find out from my lawyers that I have a meeting with the prosecutor's office. When I get there, I find out that the company I have built from the ground up, my life's work, is being charged with a crime that is unfathomable to me. The company is supposed to be humanitarian, you buffoons, and yet we are filling the ocean with garbage? That's what I heard."

I was yelling now, and I could tell that my message would be heard in my employees' nightmares for weeks. My face was beet red, and yet I didn't care. I couldn't believe what had happened all while I was on vacation enjoying champagne and women. It was too terrible to even consider. I needed a moment to compose myself before I lost my mind completely. I needed a moment to assess their worth and see if they were even worthy of continuing their employment with me.

"I need to know who did this. I pray to god it's not one of my right-hand men or women here. I would hate to think it was my very own front-runners who thought this was appropriate behavior for the company. I have one hell of a mess to clean up here. I expect you to submit reports on the hour about how you all think we should make this situation right. I want further suggestions on where the waste should go from this day forward since we now know that the ocean isn't quite the place to dump it." My voice dripped with sarcasm as I glared at my team. "Now get out of my sight."

They hurried off and out of the office as quickly as they could. I watched my team filter out of the room, hoping that my point had been made. The only other man left in the room with me was my right-hand man, Kyle, the CEO.

I stared at him a moment and he stared back, meeting my gaze unwaveringly. He had to have known something like this was going on—how could he not? But then again, I owned the whole thing, and yet I didn't know. But wasn't it his job to know the ins and outs of the company while I was away playing? That was what he was hired for after all, though I didn't think he would ever betray me in that way.

"Kyle, please tell me you had nothing to do with this. Tell me you didn't know it was happening."

Kyle was one tough son of a bitch. I had only known him to be loyal in the many years he'd worked for me. It was hard to fathom he would do something so unbelievably stupid and immoral.

"Ben, I'm shocked that you even have to ask me such a thing. We've been a team for quite some time. I assure you that I had nothing to do with this. I'm as shocked as you are about the whole thing. It's surely a minion that pulled something like that, and I promise you we'll find out who did it. That person will be punished."

"I've always appreciated your loyalty, Kyle. You've been a great asset to me as well as the company for some time. But how is it that the CEO, the guy who is supposed to have my back when I'm away, how is it that you don't know something so substantial was being done? It's madness to me that industrial waste could be dumped into the ocean and no one in the higher division has an explanation for it."

"Ben, it wasn't me. There are other people in charge of saving the company money, and this was obviously a decision that someone else made in order to do so."

I looked at him, baffled. Was he serious? "Oh yeah, of course, Kyle. What a smart idea. Of course no one would know that the company was breaking the law. Have I hired all morons? How would we not have been caught doing something like that? We would have been better to bury it in the ground. At least then it would have been harder to discover. No, instead we have to throw the shit in the ocean and kill every living thing. They have the damn vessel numbers, Kyle. It's obvious it was us, so how did we not know?" I put my head in my hands, unable to understand what was going on with the people around me.

"Look, Ben, I don't know any more about it than you do right now. But the prosecutor's office will be conducting an investigation into the matter, so we will know soon enough who was behind the whole thing."

"Are you kidding me right now?" I shouted. "I'm being charged, Kyle—do you not understand this? Do you know why? Because they think that I knew the whole time, that it was my own orders."

Kyle sighed. "Yes, I am aware. But I know you had nothing to do with the whole thing, and neither did I. They are going to discover that. You weren't even in the country for god's sake. You will prove yourself in court, and this will all go away. They can't pin something on you when you're an innocent man."

"Right, but how convenient is it that I was out of town when all this was going on? It's as if my alibi was planned."

I got up from the table and went to the window, staring out at the grand view that the boardroom held. Not quite as great as my office view but stunning nonetheless. I needed a drink. I walked to the side table where a decanter stood and poured a brandy for both me and Kyle. I returned to the table and handed Kyle the drink. I sat down beside him and sipped at the brandy, letting the heat burn down my throat, almost cleansing it.

"Kyle, I built this damn company because I believed in something. I had a dream, and this company represented that dream above anything else. Now that dream has been dragged through the mud. Our reputation is smeared and ruined completely. I don't know how we are going to turn it around. Here I am off doing charity work and fundraisers, and someone is throwing poison into the very oceans I am trying to save. It's a bloody joke."

"Ben, it's your obligation to do these works. By doing all the good that you do, you raise the money needed to make a difference. You are not expected to be around here—that's my job, and I'm sorry that something like this happened on my watch. It will be handled—I promise—and I assure you that something like this will never happen again."

"I sure hope not, because I don't think we would survive another public outcry like this one. People want my head on a chopping block."

"It will be over soon, I promise."

"What if it isn't?"

"They can't hang an innocent man, Ben. We just need to do damage control."

I held up my glass and clinked it against Kyle's. We both took another sip. I was lost in my own dark thoughts.

"How would you suggest we clean up this mess? What damage control do you have in mind?"

I could tell that Kyle was deep in thought, and I wondered if that was a good thing or a bad thing. I would do anything I could to save the reputation of this company, but I wondered what he was willing to go through in order to do the same. Kyle was now glancing out the window, and I knew I wasn't going to like what he was about to say. Kyle took another sip of the brandy, and I followed suit. When Kyle turned to me, he only said one word: "Africa."

Confused, I chuckled. "Am I supposed to know what that means?"

"Well, I've already done some research on what kind of damage control we would need at this point to salvage the reputation of not only the company, but yourself as well. We need major PR points to get through this mess. Right now, Africa is in desperate need of people to come in and build schools and hospitals. I've found a great organization that's about to start building in Malawi that could use some help. They need as many workers and supplies as possible. This is where you need to be right now, Ben—helping others and showing the world that you are the same man you were before this mess."

"Going to Africa is going to do that? It's going to fix the problem?"

"Most definitely. No one can argue the importance of all the work you have done over the years, and they won't be able to say it's an act if they see you with hammer and nails out doing it yourself. You're a billionaire—the last place they expect you to be is in Africa. We're going to send a ton of money to the job site, give them all the supplies they need, and then you will fly there and work your ass off. This will really send a message to the world as to what kind of company we are. Not to mention it will show off your strength of character in the midst of a disaster."

I mulled over what Kyle said in my head. It made sense. The last thing I had expected upon my return from vacation was to head off to Africa to work, but it was important that people not forget that I was a humanitarian at heart. I had no idea how that waste got dumped in my name, but I would never be part of such a thing. The amount of money that would have to be spent to salvage the ocean would far outweigh any profit made by the dump. Not to mention the coral and all the sea life destroyed. The thought of it all almost brought me to my knees. Going to Africa was the least that I could do to make amends for what my company did, even if I had been unaware of it all. Besides allowing me to get my hands dirty, it would also do my own soul some good. It had been a while since I had done anything quite like that, and it would help relieve the stress of what was going on. It was probably best I stay away from the company for a short while, otherwise, I might strangle someone.

I looked to Kyle and nodded. "Okay, I'm in. How do we go about doing this?"

"You leave Monday. Leave the rest up to me."

CHAPTER TWO

Ben

What I needed to bring or how much time I would be away. I did humanitarian efforts all the time, but I had never gone to a site and built a school. I had no idea how long something like that would take. I wasn't sure how much I should pack, and I suddenly wished that I had left the job up to my assistant.

I wondered what Africa was going to be like in general. Hot for sure. The people who would be involved in the building would have no idea about the scandal, and that was a good thing. I hoped to forget about it myself—the last thing I wanted was to be questioned about the whole thing. It was embarrassing enough.

It would be my first time traveling to Africa, and I had to admit I was a little excited about it. Though I had just taken a vacation, this would be something different, something from the soul. It was about time; I usually did fundraisers, but it was well past time that I got my hands dirty. None of my recent fundraisers had had anything to do with Africa, so it would be refreshing to have something new to focus on.

I considered the heat I would have to deal with there and decided only to pack light fabrics and nothing that would cling to me if I started to sweat. I smiled as I added a few more shirts to my suitcase. I was excited to work with my hands. Usually, people just wanted me to throw money at them, and although I was more than happy to do so, this little task would make me feel like a man. A masculine job that entailed putting a structure together—it didn't get much handier than that.

It amazed me that people spent their lives doing projects like that—traveling around, building hospitals for people in need. It was truly selfless. Yet, there were other people who were busy poisoning oceans. I sighed deeply. I really needed to stop thinking about the scandal, or I would surely go crazy. There was nothing I could do about it presently—I had to leave it up to Kyle and the rest of my team to clean things up at the office while I was in Africa. It would be good for me to be out with people, working together as a collective to get a job done. It wasn't just about money for me; I liked to do things that mattered. Although I had planned on getting back to work at the company after my vacation, this was what needed to be done to save the reputation of a company that was my life's work.

The project would be labor intensive, but I wasn't soft. I knew what it meant to work hard for something, and I was up for the challenge, any challenge. It was a good time to get away from the politics of the company, because something had seriously gone wrong. It would be best if I had a clear head when I returned. That way I could be more effective in righting the wrongs that were done. At this point, all I wanted to do was roar all around the office until I got some answers, and that wasn't going to do anyone any good. By going to Africa, I would be able to avoid the media as well, and the only thing they would be able to report about me was all the good I was doing on the trip. It would be really hard for them to say anything bad about me when I was trying to help people out. I could only hope that my community would be able to forgive me for the horrible error my company had made. However, that would not happen until I was able to clear my name.

I STRETCHED out my legs aboard my private jet. There would be some people who would disagree with the fact that I was flying on a private jet to an impoverished country while drinking champagne, but I usually never worried about what people thought—criminal accusations aside, of course. While I was embarking on this trip as a form of damage control and public redemption, I was also giving up a lot of my luxuries to go on this latest adventure, so I was going to enjoy them while I could. Plus, I had worked damn hard to get to where I was in life—I certainly wasn't going to apologize for it now.

Although I was going to an impoverished country, I didn't want to head over there without some of my favorite things. Some of my most favorite luxuries had been sent over so that I could indulge and also give something out to the people I met. There were cigars, chocolate, and my favorite whiskey; I couldn't imagine being gone for long periods of time without these things. I couldn't bear the thought. Some would call me spoiled, but what was the point in being a billionaire if you couldn't make life easier on yourself? I was actually looking forward to sharing my loot with everyone else there. I wasn't sure how long the other workers had been there, but they could probably use some treats at that point—something to keep them going strong.

I hoped to be there only for a few weeks. I would be getting antsy by then to get back to the company and see what was going on and whether I could be of further help there. The last thing I wanted was to be back on the sidelines, having no idea what was happening with my own company. I had made that mistake once before, and I didn't intend to make it again. I just hoped Kyle had a handle on things while I was gone. If anything else went wrong in my absence, heads were going to roll. I could promise that much.

Sitting in my seat, I sipped on the champagne and thought about the life I led and how far I had come in life. I was blessed enough to be able to come and go as I pleased, to pick up at any time and go wherever I wanted on any sort of whim. There were no attachments in my life—no wife or children, nothing to tie me down. I often reflected on these things and wondered if I was really better off without those things. I was about to turn thirty-seven, and I was still living the bachelor's life. Was that a good thing? I couldn't quite be sure.

For a very long time, I had always been happy to just focus on work. Sure, there were women in my life, but none that I fancied enough to stick around forever—they were merely a means of entertainment for me. I often liked to take women on vacation with me as the companionship was enjoyable, but again there was no real desire to see the women again once the vacation was over. It was just for fun, and for a long time that had been okay with me. In fact, rarely had I given much thought to it until recently. Things had been eating away at me for the past few months, and I wasn't sure why. My last vacation was superb, but I always got this inkling that something was missing. But was that a wife and kids? I really didn't know.

I chuckled to myself. Hell, I didn't even have a girlfriend and I was wondering if a wife would complement my life. My life was certainly in a sad state of affairs these days, and I only had myself to blame. I should never have allowed anyone else at the company to have the kind of power to issue a dumping order. I couldn't think about it without feeling sick to my stomach. Now

I was thinking about whether or not I should have a wife. Maybe this was the midlife crisis I kept hearing about. Men went through it more than women did, and I was certainly creeping in on that age. Maybe it wasn't just about having a wife. Maybe I just hadn't met the right woman yet. When she came into my life, maybe things would become clear again for me.

I took women out all the time, often to galas and benefits or a night on the town. I had even on occasion been lucky enough to cook them breakfast in the morning, but I rarely saw the same woman twice. They just didn't interest me that much. It was probably my fault; I had been unattached for so long that I wasn't sure I would know what it was like to spend long periods of time with a woman. Some women would consider me to be a player, but I didn't see it that way at all. I wasn't deliberately out to hurt anyone, and I certainly wasn't opposed to seeing a girl more than once. But she had to spike my interest, keep me intrigued—or at least be passionate about something more important than a new pair of shoes.

The kind of lady I would marry one day, if I ever did marry, would have to be able to keep me on my toes. I needed mental and physical stimulation, and I would offer the same to the woman of my choosing. I wasn't a selfish man. I didn't want a trophy wife; I wanted a woman that could stand on her own while still standing by my side when I needed her. But did such a woman exist? I wasn't sure if she did. I certainly had yet to find her.

Maybe I needed to spend less time on work and more on my personal life. Money was not an issue for me; I had enough to last many generations. My company was my empire, and it offered me a very lavish lifestyle, one that would take care of me for my entire life. I would never need to work a day in my life again if I didn't want to—of course, I would never just hand over the reins of my company, especially not after the shit show that happened that week. If anything, it appeared as if I needed a tighter grip on the reins. My presence at the company was more about having something to keep me busy—plus, I rather enjoyed being in front of the media. There was a time when I was the epitome of philanthropy and public service—that was, of course, before the media got wind that my company had been polluting the ocean.

I rubbed my temples in frustration, unable to even understand how things had gone so wrong. Maybe I should be drinking something stronger than champagne. All I could think about was strangling the idiot that made that monumental decision. If you were going to do something so stupid and thankless, why use vessels with ID numbers attached to them? How stupid could these people be? Of course, it all led back to the company, and now we were in the midst of a national scandal, one that I wasn't sure we would survive. Kyle seemed to think we would be all right, but the damage to the ocean was extensive, and there was no guarantee that we hadn't left some permanent mark.

Whoever was responsible was no doubt shaking in their boots somewhere, hoping that I would never find out. That was impossible, of course; you couldn't pull off something of that magnitude without needing some help and leaving behind a trail. Someone would come forward—if they weren't discovered first. Who knew what was going through this fool's mind? For all I knew, the person might have thought that I would be okay with it. Maybe even applaud him for his genius. There were fake humanitarians all over the world, but I wasn't one of them. I would never be okay with disposing of waste in such a manner.

"Mr. Donovan, would you like more champagne? Your dinner will be out shortly."

I looked up, snapped out of my thoughts. "Yes, of course, thank you. Can I have something a little stiffer though?"

The girl smiled a smile that revealed a lot more than just her happiness to get me another drink. The look she was giving me said she wanted something a little stiffer too. I appraised her, noticing her natural beauty and responding to it. I certainly could use a release and wished I could take her to the back cabin and take her right there. But I had a strict rule against sleeping with staff—it was a terrible idea and always had a way of biting you in the ass, and not in a good way. I didn't need any more scandals in my life, so my staff was always off-limits. The last thing I needed was an angry employee out to seek revenge on me. No, that was something I did not need. The press I was getting now alone was killing me. At the end of the day, it just wasn't worth it to sleep with an employee. It's not like I had trouble finding female companionship, so employees were easy to stay away from.

Plus, I could never be sure if I was being hit on because someone liked me or because they wanted to be Mrs. Billionaire. If you were gonna get married, then why not aim to marry a billionaire? It would be quite a prize for the right girl, and when it came to my staff, I often wondered if they just saw me as a means of moving up in the world. I hated thinking that way, but in my world, it happened all the time. Trophy wives were the thing to have, but no thank you. I had no interest in that at all.

The stewardess returned with my drink looking mildly sulky. She had expected me to take her up on her advances, and when I didn't, she took it personally. That was the dangerous part. She would have been trouble had we slept together and I wronged her. I smiled at her warmly, hoping to ease her wounded ego. The girl was an absolute fox; it was nothing personal, just business. She smiled back at me and hurried off. She wasn't gone long before she returned with my dinner for the evening. The meal looked incredible: grilled salmon and asparagus with small potatoes. I downed the brandy in one gulp, letting it burn my throat on the way down, and then I focused my full attention on the meal before me. The stewardess returned one more time to refill my champagne glass, and then she flitted away.

Most of my favorite meals usually included some form of seafood. I couldn't seem to get enough of it. When it came to maintaining my lean physique, I believed in trying to eat as clean as possible with some treats thrown in here and there. It was just as important to my business and successful lifestyle that I kept my body running smoothly as well—that was how you prevented disease from sneaking in, and when you're building a top company, you can't afford to take sick days. The mind and body always had to be in harmony, and it was my job to take care of that to the best of my ability.

After I devoured the food before me, I suddenly felt exhausted. The goings-on at the company had been of significant mental strain to me, and I was mentally tapped out. I needed a little siesta, and then I would be back in business. I figured it was best to get a nap in while I was still on the jet. Once I arrived in Malawi, I wasn't sure that there would be time for one. I positioned my seat so that it leaned back all the way into a bed.

As I lay back, the stewardess made her way back to me with a pillow and a blanket. It was bizarre watching someone essentially tuck me in for the night, but it was also quite nice. It was the closest I had gotten to true companionship in some time, something that would naturally happen if I'd had a girlfriend. The last thought I had before I closed my eyes was to wonder what it would feel like to have someone in my life that I could take care of and who I knew would also take care of me.

WHEN THE PLANE LANDED, the first thing that hit me when I stepped out was the heat. I knew it would be hot, but I hadn't quite expected this level of heat. I was really in for it, and I was lucky I had done a thorough job of packing.

Malawi was just as beautiful as it was hot. Everywhere I looked it was as if I were on a whole different planet. There was a natural beauty to the place I just didn't see back home—no skyscraper buildings to block the view of what nature had in store for me.

Once we landed, I was ushered through the tiny airport and shuttled to the site at which I would be working. The first thing they did was bring me to the cabin where I would be staying. I wanted to unpack and get settled before things really got crazy for me.

When I arrived at the cabin, I was truly in awe of everything. I couldn't have been happier that I had decided to go on this little adventure and hoped the whole experience would be worthwhile and beneficial for all. The cabin assigned to me had a porch that made me smile immediately. There was something about the thought of working hard all day and then returning to that cabin to an evening whiskey on the porch that filled me with contentment. I could already picture it. It would be marvelous. The cabin was nowhere near luxurious, but it had everything I needed for my stay there.

My first plan of attack was to get unpacked, and then I could take a look around at the site and meet the people in charge. I would get a feel for things that day and then get started with the team the next day. I was pleased to see that all my packages had already arrived. I wanted my belongings and luxury items on hand at all times. I went through the packages and noticed that Kyle had also sent wine, probably just in case I wasn't dining alone. Kyle always thought ahead, and I liked that about him. If I managed to dine alone, I could always give the bottles away. The thing that brought the biggest smile to my face was the bags and bags of individually wrapped candy that I could pass out to any children that I saw. I knew it would make their faces light up as nothing else would.

Once my unpacking was completed, I ventured out onto the porch and took a look around. The heat was therapeutic and made one feel like there was nothing wrong in the world. It wasn't quite the same as lying out on the beach or riding around on my yacht, but the feeling of being in the heat was still very enjoyable. There was a wooden lawn chair on the porch, and I sat down in it. I yawned as I stretched my hands above my head. Yes, there was a lot of good that could be done in a place like this, and I intended on doing what I could while I was there.

The forest surrounding my cabin was lush, a green so bright that it almost hurt to look at the trees. I couldn't believe that such places existed in the world. I just didn't see places like that where I was from. New York really was a concrete jungle compared to this place. I felt blessed to be there and to be in the position where I could help others. I would be able to do a lot of good for the village, and I couldn't wait to get started.

There was a hammock attached to one of the trees, and the sight of it pleased me greatly. I could imagine retiring in it at the end of a grueling day of hammering nails in the heat. I smiled as I thought about the last time I was in a hammock. It must have been when I was a young boy, probably behind my grandparents' place—there was a hammock by the pond. I used to go back there and lay for hours in it, letting the breeze float around me. My own parents had died when I was around ten years old, and I had been raised by an aunt for the most part, often spending time at my grandparents' place. The circumstances of my childhood probably had a lot to do with the fact that I didn't have a lot of attachments to other people.

Well, it was time that I got moving and introduced myself to the people running the site. I doubted I would be working that day, but I wasn't too worried about it either way. If they needed me right away, I would do what I could. Excitement boiled up in me as I thought about making my way to the site and seeing how far along the school and hospital were. I got up from the seat and grabbed a bottle of water before I made my way down the stairs. I followed a path through the lush forest toward what I hoped was the building site. I hadn't seen anyone since I had been dropped off at the cabin, but they had left on the path, so I knew I would find someone eventually.

I was anxious to talk to the head honcho about what the expectations were for me. All the supplies for the site had been paid for by my company and shipped ahead of time, so I wanted to check to make sure they'd gotten everything they needed. It took a lot of supplies to build those two structures, and money meant very little to me—I had plenty to go around and wouldn't miss it.

Thankful for the hat I brought, I could already feel myself building up a sweat as I walked along the path. The sun was beating down even through the trees, and there was not much escape from it. It felt good though; it wasn't overbearing in the least. There was none of the humidity that I was used to during the summer months. The heat was dry, so it never felt as hot as it actually was. In fact it was downright soothing.

The path broke open onto the building site, which was overflowing with people. There was movement and action all around me, and it excited me even more. Everyone was clearly very busy, and a moment was never wasted. The energy in the place was inspiring. There were local villagers around, sitting and watching the volunteers building. It looked as if they were checking out the new people coming and going. The local villagers looked happy, as if they loved the new visitors coming in to change things and hopefully make them better.

I stood on the edge of everything, watching as volunteers unpacked and sorted through the supplies I had sent. I was impressed to see they already had the school's frame well underway. It was already starting to look like something. I felt pride for the camp and what they had accomplished in such a short amount of time, and now I would be part of it. I was going to be able to make a difference, and that was all that mattered to me. As far as I was concerned, the media could kiss my ass. There was no way anyone could believe that I was involved in poisoning the ocean—it truly was ludicrous.

"Mr. Donovan, welcome to the site! We are so happy to have you."

I was startled by a voice beside me and I turned to find a rather pale-looking man. Considering we were in Africa, I was shocked that anyone could remain pale skinned, but sure enough, the man had the pallor of a vampire. His cheeks, however, were flushed, which gave the indication that maybe he just didn't do that well in the heat and hot temperatures. It was a mystery, however, as to why his skin just didn't tan or at least burn. Instead it looked like it lacked almost all color. I put on a warm smile and shook the sweaty palm of the man in front of me.

"Hello, are you the man in charge? I just got here and thought I would take a look around."

"Yes I am, as a matter of fact. The name is Paul, and it is quite a pleasure to meet you. Everyone is so excited that you have decided to join us in our ventures. We couldn't be more grateful for the supplies you sent us. It was very generous of you. As you can see, we are well on our way to having a school, thanks to you."

"The pleasure is all mine, and yes, I did notice that. It looks great and I'm glad to have helped. And please, call me Ben. There is no need to be formal."

"Indeed you are right about that. I am head of the project here, and if there is anything that you require, please come and see me. We have many projects going, all of which are running smoothly. I've been in Africa for over a year now running various projects all over the continent through the very company that you contacted in order to join us here. Were you able to get settled in the cabin?"

"Yes, it's great, thank you. I'm looking forward to getting involved here. I don't think I'll be able to stay as long as you have, but I'll do my best for as long as I'm here," I said with a chuckle.

"Great, that's all good news. Again, we are grateful that you have come to help. There is certainly much to do."

"I wasn't sure if you needed me to start up today or if I would begin in the morning. It's been a taxing day of travel."

"That's totally up to you. Now, what kind of work are you interested in?"

I took a look around. Since my arrival to the site, I felt invigorated and decided to get going right away; there was no need to wait until the morning. Besides, I would only be putting a few hours in before the site shut down for the day and people went off to dinner.

"I'm at your disposal, and I think I'd like to do some work today after all. I'm okay with getting dirty as well—you don't need to give me any special treatment."

Paul laughed. "Good man. That's what I like to hear. How are you with using a hammer?"

"Great. Just show me what you need."

Just then there was a tugging on my leg, and I looked down to see a little girl with chocolate-brown eyes. She was tugging on my pant leg trying to get my attention. She was very skinny, though she didn't appear to be malnourished in any way. I smiled down at her and said, "Hi there, how are you?" The girl smiled back up at me, and I wasn't sure if she understood me at all.

"This is one of our most frequent visitors. Plenty of the children from the nearby villages wander over from time to time. Everyone is very excited that the school is being built, for obvious reasons."

"Do they not have a school?"

"They do and you will see more children filter through during their breaks, but the school is rundown. If there is ever a hard rain, the school floods, and it's not nearly big enough for the number of children in it. They need an upgrade, and this school will mean the ability to learn without worrying about the school falling apart around them. So yes, I believe this little one should be in school, but they get so excited that some venture over whether they are allowed to or not."

I chuckled. "That's fine by me. I'm looking forward to visiting the villages and meeting everyone."

"I'm sure that they would love that. Come with me."

I followed Paul over to a group of people that he introduced me to. It was obvious by the looks they were giving me that they all knew that I was the billionaire funding the project. Not that it bothered me; I would win them over eventually. I just needed to have faith in the situation. I was used to that treatment wherever I went even in the Upper East Side. People treat you differently when you're rich. I was considered one of the elite, and usually everyone wanted a piece of me in more ways than one. But in New York, I was treated with respect automatically. In places like Africa on a job site, I needed to earn the respect first.

It was no big deal though. I was confident that in a few days they would see me as I really was and warm up to me. I was no snob, and they would see that soon enough.

"Now that you've met everyone, Ben, how about we put you to work?"

"Sounds good to me."

The people were smiling around me, but I knew they were

anxious to see if I could actually do hard labor. What they didn't know was that my grandfather used to be a farmer, and I often helped him out on the weekends when I didn't have school. I hadn't always had a privileged life; I had worked hard to get where I am. I followed Paul to where all the tools were being stored. I was handed a hammer and a few boxes of nails.

"You can start over there and work with that group. They'll show you exactly what to do. I'll check on you in a bit, okay?"

"Great, and thanks a lot." I headed to the group, who showed me how they were framing the school. I got to work immediately, hammering nails into the structure, creating a frame as we went along.

There was no doubt about it, the work was truly soul-cleansing, and I knew that going there had been a great idea indeed. The hard work was exactly what I needed to exorcise my demons. I took out all my pent-up aggression on those boards, nailing them in deeper and deeper. I knew I was where I was supposed to be, and when the work was done, I would have a clear head and know exactly what was to be done about my company and the people in it. All the pain and anger from the past week were going into the boards, and I started to feel a weight being lifted off me. By the time Paul came back to retrieve me, we had completely finished the framing of the school, and it looked amazing.

I stood up and joined the people staring at the hard work from the day. I was sweating buckets, but I felt alive for the first time in a long time.

"Great job, everyone. This looks great," I said.

There were lots of high fives and slaps on the back to go around for everyone. They were all pretty proud of the performance that day, and I couldn't blame them. It was amazing what you could do when you had people working together as a team to get a job done. That was a perfect example right there.

As I looked around, I had a great idea. Why not end off my first day there with a bang, something that would make everyone feel wonderful for all the work that was put in that day.

"Excuse me, everyone. It would be my honor if you would all join me at my cabin for dinner tonight. Arrangements have been made for a great spread to be there tonight, and I would love it if you would all join me in having a celebration feast for a job well done. You deserve it, and I hope to see you all there. If the food isn't enough to get you there, I also have alcohol."

There was collective laughter all around, and the sound of it pleased me greatly. They all started to cheer, which made me laugh. "Okay, let's meet at my cabin in an hour. I need to wash off all this sweat."

The crowd started to part, and I made my way back toward the pathway when I was stopped by a kid who couldn't have been more than nineteen. I had been introduced to him before; his name might have been Jeff.

"Hi, Ben. I was just wondering, since you invited us all to dinner and all..."

"Yes?"

"Well, there is another site, the one where they are putting up the hospital. We all usually get together for dinner at the end of the day. Would it be okay if I invited them as well?"

"Of course. We're all in this together after all. I say the more, the merrier."

The kid smiled brightly. "Thanks, man. You are one pretty cool guy."

"Yeah, thanks," I said with a laugh.

CHAPTER THREE

Ben

There were plenty of tables set outside the cabin, and most of them were filled with food from the nearest town. Everything was hot and smelled fantastic. No one was late, probably because you could smell the food for miles and everyone was famished after a hard day's work. I walked around and personally introduced myself to everyone. I wanted them to feel at home with me and not feel like it was a formal affair.

As I was making my rounds, my eyes caught sight of a beautiful woman, her skin lightly tanned. She was easily the most beautiful woman I had ever seen, and her beauty appeared to be natural. She had long, curly red hair tied up in a messy bun that looked sexier than if she had it curled for a gala event. Even from a distance, I could tell she had startling green eyes that seemed to draw in people all around her. She had pouty, sensual lips that looked like they were just begging to be kissed. She looked exotic, though I knew her to be an American as well. She was breathtaking, and it took all my effort to not just stand there and stare at her.

I couldn't tell her age, not that it really mattered to me. All I was able to focus on was how her smile seemed to light up the whole area. Who was that beautiful creature? She must have been from the hospital site because I knew I would have remembered her from my own site. I probably would have followed her around all day. She was with a few friends, chatting amiably and looking around at the feast in amazement.

She was tall and had the build of a professional dancer. I knew I had to try to focus on something else because I was having a hard time taking my eyes off her. She was a stunner, and yet all she wore was cargo pants and a tank top. Even in her plain clothes she could knock the socks off any high-society girl from New York. She was eyeing up the food with her friends, and I was suddenly more pleased than ever that I had arrived the whole thing. The volunteers probably hadn't eaten that well in a while, and I may not have had the chance to meet the girl had I not arranged such a dinner. Whether or not the groups collided in their work, I didn't know, but this event allowed me to make my own introductions to her. I wasn't about to waste any time getting to know her; I didn't want anyone else swooping in before I had the chance to speak with her.

I moved toward her immediately, almost knocking down a few volunteers in the process.

"So sorry," I muttered as I made my way through the crowd.

The closer I got to her, the more beautiful she became—if that were possible. I slowly approached the group she was in as they were gathering up food on their plates. I was close enough to touch her, and I could smell her perfume. It was like sandalwood, and the smell made me want to pull her close to me.

"Hi there. Would you guys care for something to drink?"

She turned to me and smiled, and that was the best gift I

could have been given that day. Her eyes sparkled when she smiled, and it took all my willpower not to pull her in for a kiss. Those lips—I wanted to claim them. I had never reacted in such a way around a woman. I was usually very cool about talking to women, but this one made me think only of my bedroom and what I could do to her there.

"Hi. Ben, is it? We've heard a lot about you. Thank you for inviting us to this party. Everything looks delicious. I'm Katie and I work with the AIDS education initiative. We help people in the villages all around here."

So she wasn't from the other building site. Well, the more, the merrier was what I liked to say. I welcomed all the volunteers to come.

"Katie, that's a pretty name. I'm glad that you could come, all of you."

She blushed and I liked the way her cheeks reddened. It made her even more beautiful.

"I'm famished. I was so thrilled to find out we had a place to go where there was already food ready. I don't even know where to begin."

"Oh, you are very welcome. Food has also been sent to the villages. They should enjoy the festivities as well."

She smiled widely. "Well, that's very sweet of you. I'm sure a hearty meal will do everyone good." She was looking at me with interest, and I wondered if anyone would notice if I snatched her away. I wanted to bring her into the cabin and touch every inch of her.

"Oh, it was nothing. I'm happy to do it."

We stared at each other for a moment, and I wondered if she was feeling the same way that I was. There was a current of electricity charging through my body with her being in such close proximity. It was like we were the only two people there. I didn't even care to talk to anyone else but her. She captivated me, and I wanted to put my mouth on her, badly. She was staring back at me unwaveringly, and I had to wonder if she was having some dirty thoughts herself.

"Well, it was really nice to meet you, Katie."

I held out my hand, and she took it. I shook her hand for an inappropriately long time. We were still staring at each other when I heard her friends giggling. The spell broken, I dropped her hand. Katie was smiling as I tried to compose myself.

"How about that drink?"

She nodded and I proceeded to pour a glass for both her and her friends. I excused myself immediately, not wanting to overstay my welcome. I had no idea what was going through her head, but I knew I needed to clear mine. I went about getting myself a plateful of food and went to find Paul.

Paul was sitting at a table with a few others, and I decided to join them. While I sat there eating, I realized I didn't have much to say. Paul was certainly making up for it as he chatted with everyone, telling all kinds of stories. I was grateful for it because I didn't feel like I could hold my own in a conversation at that point.

The food was fantastic, of course. There were various types of meat, from chicken to ribs to sausages, and a mixture of vegetables and potatoes. There were also various salads and fresh fruit for the taking. It was quite a feast indeed, and everything was fresh. As I ate, however, I had a hard time focusing on anything but my conversation with Katie. We hadn't talked much; it was more about the feeling she gave me when we talked. I kept glancing in her general direction to see what she was doing. She was a bundle of light no matter what she did. She was talking animatedly with her friends, and she seemed like the type of person who really loved life, and that was refreshing to see. I knew I had to have her no matter what. I had never felt such an instant connection to any other woman, and I was determined to make her mine.

As the night wore on, I kept my eye on her and thought of what I could do to win her over. I had caught her eye a few times, and I suspected she had been looking around for me as well. The very thought made me a little hard when I considered that she might want me as badly as I wanted her. All I could think about was undressing her and spreading her legs before me. I needed to find out more about her, see if anyone knew her personally.

I glanced at Paul, who was sipping on some whiskey. "Hey, how well do you know the volunteers that work with AIDS?"

"Oh, very well. I make it a point to know everyone around here. At some point, we end up becoming one big family."

"That's good, especially for those that stay on for long periods of time. What's the story with Katie?"

Paul chuckled. "Are you interested in the girl? You certainly wouldn't be the first man to try to catch her eye. She's gorgeous, which is why there seems to be so much interest in her, of course. Despite that fact, she hasn't shown any interest in anyone else since she's been here. She keeps to herself a lot. I think she's pretty private about her life."

I nodded, taking it all in. "She's not actually a girl, is she?"

Paul couldn't help but laugh out loud, drawing attention to our table. Katie glanced my way, and our eyes locked. I held her gaze for a beat, feeling aroused all over again. What was with this woman and the power she had over me?

"No, of course not. Though we do get some volunteers who are young, I think she's around twenty-eight and quite a bright girl. As far as I know, she's taking a break from her life to find herself a bit before going back to the real world. But I guess that's what we're all doing here, isn't it, Ben?"

I met his gaze and knew that he had heard all about the

scandal going on back home at my company. I wondered who told him and whether others at the site knew about it as well. I supposed it was bound to happen no matter what, but I had hoped for a little time off from discussing it. I could only hope that Paul, and whoever else knew, didn't think badly of me. I would at least like the benefit of the doubt in the situation. I had, after all, done nothing wrong. The last thing I wanted was for anyone to believe the rumors about me. It was a horrible situation, and I didn't like the idea that I could come to a place like Africa for a break only to have it all follow me there.

I nodded slowly. "Yeah, you're right. That's usually why people find themselves in a place like this. Working off their sins, I suppose, or trying to save the world, yet sometimes I think the two are often connected."

"True enough, Ben. I can tell you are a good man though."

"I appreciate that, Paul. As are you."

Paul smiled and picked up his plate as he left the table. People started filtering out for the evening, the sun long gone now, leaving behind the moon for company. It was time for everyone to retire for the night as work started again at 6 a.m. I knew what I had to do; I wasn't the kind of man that believed in having regrets. I stood up from my table and threw my plate in the garbage. I then made my way over to the table that Katie was in the middle of leaving.

"Katie, I wondered if you would like to stick around and have another drink with me?"

She smiled warmly, and her friends giggled beside her. They left immediately, knowing full well what Katie was going to say. It made me wonder if I had been the topic of conversation at their table for the evening.

"That would be wonderful, thank you. You can't keep me out late though—I'm not a morning person and I need my beauty sleep." She laughed as she said it, and I had never heard anything more pleasing.

"I doubt that." I motioned for her to head up to the porch, and she did so, finding herself a seat against the railing. I went ahead and poured us both a glass of wine and handed her one. She took a sip and looked out at the night. The sounds all around us were nothing like what you would hear in the city; it was actually kind of magical. I sat down beside her, ignoring the chair. I didn't want to be that far away from her.

"Tell me, Katie, what brought you to Africa? Tell me more about the AIDS volunteer work you are doing."

"Well, for the most part it's education based. We spend most of our time at the current school teaching the kids. AIDS is a real problem here, and we hope to try to stop it from affecting future generations. We are trying to teach the kids about sex and how the disease is spreading out of control. We hope to prevent it from happening. At this point, all we can do is educate them and tell them how to avoid it."

"I'm surprised that such a young girl is so invested in a project like this."

"I'm not that young," she said with a laugh. She stared at me long enough to drive her point home. Every part of my body took the hint.

"I just meant that someone as young as you should be out enjoying her youth, going out and having fun with friends and going to parties."

"Well, I did do all that, but that stuff gets old. I want my life to have a purpose. I don't want to be club-hopping all through my twenties."

I nodded, watching her carefully. Paul was right; she had a good head on her shoulders.

"So why come here?"

She turned to me. "No, you first. We all know you to be quite a wealthy man, Ben. What brings you to Africa to slum with the rest of us?"

I chuckled. "It's hardly slumming it. Something unexpected happened at my company recently that really had me reevaluating a lot of things. Trouble is brewing, I'm afraid, and I needed a break from it all. This is my temporary escape, somewhere that I can do some good while allowing myself to get a clear perspective on things. Plus, it was time that I got my hands dirty for a change instead of constantly writing checks. It's nice to come and meet a situation head on instead of just throwing money at it. By being here, I can truly see what's going on and where I can help the most."

"Yeah, I can understand that. Well, to some degree—I don't think I have any idea what it's like to be in charge of a billion-dollar company. Your lifestyle is very different from mine, I'm sure."

"Maybe." I smiled. "Now it's your turn."

She looked into her hands, suddenly looking very sad. "I came here because I realized I had an amazing life, and I felt guilty for it. Sounds crazy, I know. All my friends back home thought I was nuts, but I've just been so blessed in life that I wanted to make my life matter more, I guess."

"Interesting. Explain it to me."

She smiled and took a deep breath, looking quite wistful about what she was going to say. "Oh, there's no terrible past haunting me or anything. People just look at my life and think I should have this whole journey attached to it, and I don't."

"What sort of story do they expect you to have?"

She laughed. "I guess I'm not really explaining myself very well, am I?"

I smiled.

"Well, my family is completely normal and all well educated. A lot of people here are running away from something. I'm not.

My life is normal and happy. I'm educated as well. I went to university for fashion, and that's what I plan on focusing on when I get back. I already have clients lined up waiting for my designs. Some weren't too happy that I decided to take a hiatus."

"You sound like you have a promising future, so I'm not sure what you feel guilty about."

She giggled. "I didn't expect you to be so easy to talk to." I smiled at her, glad that she found comfort in talking to me. I had to admit that I enjoyed talking with her as well.

"Hold your thought while I pour us some more wine." I left her sitting on the porch while I went to fetch another bottle of wine. I didn't fill the glasses too much this time, as I didn't want her to be hungover in the morning and it was getting late. I returned to the porch and handed her the glass.

"I hope you don't feel guilty about being successful, Katie, because that's something that you are supposed to take pride in."

"I knew a girl once who had to struggle for everything she had. When we were in school together, she wrote a paper on the African American culture. It was rather beautiful." She paused and I waited for her to finish. I was completely intrigued by her; I could listen to her talk like that all night, even though I couldn't help but think how much fun other things could be as well.

"I guess knowing this girl is where the guilt comes in for me. She ended up going into politics while I studied fashion. We got together once, and she ended up showing me a video of the things that were going on in Africa. She is a big advocate, and she wanted me to be more involved in the world than just fashion. It made me realize how much I had in life while there were others who had nothing at all. Do you know what I mean? I just knew that I needed to give something back, to try to make a difference even if it was just in some small way. So I left my sister in charge of the ordering of my designs, and I imagine by the time I get back I'll have a whole fashion company in the works. Which of course is very exciting."

"You have a lot to be proud of, I hope you realize that. Your parents must be very happy with you."

"Actually, no, they're not at all right now. They worked really hard in their life to give me a better life, something grander than the one that they had. They wanted me to enjoy the life they gave me, not come here and feel guilty about it," she said with a laugh.

"I guess I can understand that. Parents always want what's best for their kids, and they just want you to be successful. This is temporary, of course, and they will see you happy in your business and the rest won't matter."

"Thank you for saying that."

I chuckled, not wanting the talk to get too serious. I was surprised by how the conversation had turned. I wasn't exactly the type of person that liked to dig deep when I first met someone—of course, things just felt different with Katie.

"Well, you can't be much older than I am," she uttered.

"A little bit. I'm thirty-six. Plus, I have a lot of experience, probably more so than you."

"Experience in what?" she whispered. It wasn't so much that she whispered but how she whispered that caught me off guard. It was like she had lost her breath—it was kind of hot. I didn't know what to say to her; she had rendered me speechless. I felt like I was losing control of my thoughts and wasn't sure that it was the right time to make a move on her.

"I really feel like you understand me, Ben, and that's a rare thing to find. You make me want to tell you things that I shouldn't."

She was looking up into my eyes. "Oh, I definitely like you too, probably more than I should."

"Well, we don't always have to be good, do we? We can just follow how we feel, can't we?"

I stared into those insanely green eyes as they bore into mine. I could feel myself growing hard, and my eyes found her lips. All I wanted to do was take her right then and there, put my hot mouth on her body. We had just met, and I worried we would be starting something we couldn't finish. I didn't want to hurt her. I wasn't exactly used to having attachments. And though we wouldn't be working together exactly, we would be working close by, and I didn't want to cause a mess with the important work we were both doing. The last thing I needed were rumors going around about the two of us. The problem, however, was that all I could do was think about how good it would feel to slide inside of her. I didn't think I would be able to get that thought out of my head.

"I should tell you, Ben, that no man has been able to give me an orgasm before."

Before I could process what she just said to me, she got up and made the decision for me. She latched her mouth on to mine, and the fire that lit between us was intense. Katie gasped inside my mouth, and my loins burned for her. My hands went into her hair, pulling her closer to me. I kissed her deeply, finding her tongue and sucking on it gently. She moaned and the sounds she made had me rock hard in a second. Oh yes, I would have her tonight. I needed to hear her moan all night long.

I stood up then and pulled her body to mine. I kissed down to her chin and trailed kisses along her neck, sucking on her. Her hands found the bulge in my shorts, rubbing me hard, causing a friction that drove me insane. The knowledge that she was eager for my cock drove me half-mad. I picked her up, carrying her into the cabin, and laid her out on my bed.

I pulled off her tank top and unclasped her bra. Her breasts dropped deliciously from the bra, and I bent down to suck on her nipples. She gave a guttural moan and I sucked even harder. I planned on giving her an orgasm she would never forget. I couldn't believe that she had never had one before. Who were these men she was sleeping with? She was so responsive; the other guys she'd been with must've been totally clueless.

She pushed me away to tear off her shorts, and I glimpsed a pair of white lace panties before she slid them to the floor. I couldn't believe how badly I wanted to fuck her right then. She drove me insane.

I dropped to the floor in front of her, spreading her legs as she leaned back on the bed. Her pussy was so pink it made me crazy. She was already wet, and I slid a finger inside her, feeling her drip down my finger. I bent forward, placing my lips on her clit. She gasped in surprise as my lips touched her pussy. I loved the taste of her, and I drank in her juices as I felt them against my mouth.

I licked her like she was the tastiest ice cream and plunged my tongue inside her. I ached to fuck her, but having this taste of her was hard to pass up. I licked her pussy all over; having her cum in my mouth would be the ultimate victory. I moaned deeply. Licking her pussy made me so horny.

"Katie, you are so hot. I love this."

She writhed against me, and I knew I had to have her soon.

"Oh my god, Ben." She moaned my name, and it was just about the best sound I had ever heard. I leaned in and sucked her clit, forcing her to thrash beneath me. "Right there, baby, that feels so good." Katie made a high-pitched sound I had never heard before, and knowing I brought her so much pleasure had me bound and determined to give her the elusive orgasm she'd never had with a man.

"I'm so close... oh god..." Katie grabbed the back of my head and pushed up harder against my mouth. I sucked her good while fucking her with my finger.

With an earth-shattering scream, Katie came all over my finger and mouth. I pulled out and looked into her dazed eyes. Her face was flushed from her orgasm, and I felt a swelling sense of pride and satisfaction. Knowing I was the only man to ever bring her to that state made me harder than I'd ever been in my life. I wanted my cock in her pussy the next time she came.

Katie panted heavily, trying to catch her breath, but she couldn't have made it clearer that she wanted the same thing as I did with the next words that came out of her mouth. "Please, Ben, I want you inside me."

I never wanted a lady to beg. I would give her exactly what she wanted. I pulled Katie up and turned her over. She gasped in excitement as she bent over for me, her tight round bottom in my face. I bent down and kissed her bottom, moving in real close to her. I was rock hard and couldn't wait to plunge inside her pink little pussy.

I drove deep inside her, making her moan loudly. She was tight and wet, and I really had to control myself or I would lose myself completely inside her.

"Ben, I need it."

Her ass looked glorious before me as I plunged deeper inside and moved within her. She called out to me loudly, and I briefly wondered if there was anyone within earshot. I couldn't have cared less, however—let the whole village hear us. I was fucking an amazing woman, and I wouldn't stop for anything.

Katie was so sensitive from her first orgasm that she came against my cock with a couple of thrusts. I continued to rock inside her until I spilled into her as well. I leaned down on top of her back, breathing heavily into her hair.

"Oh, Katie that was incredible."

"You bet your ass it was." She giggled underneath me. I

rolled off her and lay down on the bed. She lay beside me, and we were both silent, thinking about what had just happened between us. She rolled onto my chest and nuzzled into it. I wrapped my hands around her and kissed her on the top of her head.

"Yes, that definitely was amazing." We fell asleep tangled up in each other's arms.

CHAPTER FOUR

Ben

The next morning, I awoke well before dawn and felt a beautiful woman in my arms. I pulled her in tighter and felt myself grow hard again. I wasn't sure what was going to happen between us after the night we'd had together, but I didn't want to pass up morning sex with her. It was the best way to start the day after all, and there weren't too many women that could make me hard instantly. I wanted to fuck her before we went off to work. I nuzzled into her neck until I felt her stir. She moaned as I pressed my hard cock against her bottom.

"I need you badly, Katie. My god, it hasn't even been twenty-four hours and I need to be inside you right now. I would love to give you more orgasms—I know you've been denied them for far too long."

Her breath caught and she couldn't even respond to me. What a turn-on to have a woman react to me in that way, to show me that she needed me that much. My body was warm all over at the thought of taking her again.

She turned over to me and kissed me, her tongue sliding gently into my mouth and touching my tongue. Electricity hit me and I started to feel hot. Oh god, what was with this girl? She was just so incredible that I couldn't keep my hands off her, and I was sure she felt exactly the same way.

She smiled up at me again, her eyes watching me intensely. "I would like you to touch me."

I groaned. "Baby, that's all I want to do. I want to have that sweet ass in my hands once again. You are so hot, Katie."

She moaned. "Oh Ben, that is so sexy. I love the way you talk to me."

She moved closer to me and rubbed the front of my underwear, pressing her hand against my cock. Talk about easy access. She was kneading hard against me until I felt myself growing harder still. I had already been plenty hard when I woke up, and feeling myself grow turned me on that much more. She could make me rock hard so easily. I groaned at her touch, and my hands slowly went down her body and grasped her ass.

I smiled. "I can't help myself. I just can't get enough of you."

"I know how you feel." She giggled.

She raised herself in the doggy position. She knew exactly what she wanted.

"You want me to fuck you from behind? I'm going to make you feel incredible."

Her firm ass was there for me to take, and I wanted to slip in from behind nice and deep. She was completely perfect. I couldn't take it; I wanted to pound her hard from behind and make her say my name again and again.

I was going to fuck her really good. I squeezed her breasts from underneath, and she released a soft cry. My head was filled with this girl, and I knew I wouldn't have been able to go to the site that day and try to work without dipping my cock into her first.

My fingers found her opening. I loved how she was always ready for me, her pussy wet with need for me. "Oh baby, you are already so wet."

I plunged a finger inside her and fucked her gently while she mewled in my arms. I was already addicted to her, and I needed to fuck her more than anything. I knew she felt exactly the same way; I could practically feel her need for me. She made me lose all sense of reasoning—it was like there was a fog that surrounded us when she was around and she was all that mattered. She wanted me and she was going to get all of me. I lifted her up and flipped her over.

"Don't worry, sweetheart, I'm going to fuck you good doggy-style—I just want something first."

She lay back onto the bed and spread her legs. Seeing her wet pussy right there before me almost drove me half-mad. She looked good enough to eat, and I planned on licking every inch of her soaking pussy. I bent down and started to slowly lick her opening, sticking my tongue inside of her.

"Baby, you are so hot."

She writhed against me, and I knew I had to have her, to fuck her really good. I sat up and pulled her up to me. She turned around and leaned forward, her firm ass high in the air as I slid inside her warm pussy and felt the deepness. I groaned with pleasure. She felt amazing and I doubted that I would ever tire of having my cock inside of her. I was so deep—I couldn't believe how incredible she felt.

"Harder, Ben, please."

That was all it took. I pumped against her hard, feeling every inch of her. Her fingers clenched against the bed sheets as waves of pleasure went through her. She called out my name over and over again, and it was music to my ears. She wanted it hard, and I would bet she would be sore later—I would guarantee that much. I fucked her hard, listening to her whimper my name. I pumped harder while I reached over and rubbed her clit. She was so wet that my fingers slid over her pussy easily. I bent forward and kissed her shoulder, nipping it gently. I fondled her breasts from underneath, loving the feel of her soft skin.

I could feel her tightening around me, and I knew she was going to cum again. I pumped faster and she muffled her cries of pleasure into the pillows. Oh, she was good, really good. Her orgasm broke through, and she whimpered as she finished. I continued to thrust into her; I wasn't ready to give up yet.

I rubbed her ass while I was still inside her. "You truly are a gift to me, Katie. I can't get enough of you."

I pulled out of her and she quickly flipped over, surprising me. She pushed me back down on the bed and straddled me. It was the hottest sight I had seen in some time. I couldn't believe it was possible, but I was growing even harder watching her. She bent down and took my cock into her mouth. I moaned as she sucked hard.

"Whoa! Baby, easy, or you are going to make me cum." I almost lost control. She sucked me hard, and I whispered, "What an amazing blow job, baby." Her tongue swirled around my cock as she took me in deeper into her mouth, my cock hitting the back of her throat. I groaned as she made my cock start to throb. She continued sucking until I begged her to stop.

"C'mon, baby, I want to fuck you again." She rose from her position and kissed me on the mouth. Her mouth on me was hot and wet. I slid my hand to her pussy and rubbed at her clit.

"Oh, sweetheart, you are so wet."

"Oh Ben, you do that to me. I can't stop thinking about you inside me. I just have to have you again. And it's my turn to make you feel good."

I smiled, loving the way she talked to me. When she talked dirty, it drove me wild. We were kindred spirits.

"I can't wait to fuck you again, Katie. I was so disappointed to have to leave your pussy." I went to lift her up onto my cock when she stopped me. I sat back but she pushed me right back down. I laughed, enjoying the look on her face. She had the power now, and she was enjoying every bit of it. I looked her up from top to bottom, finally resting my eyes on her perfectly shaved pussy. My cock was hard and ready, and she knew I didn't want to wait any longer. She climbed on top of me and kissed me passionately, and my hands found her breasts.

She was blowing my mind. "You want to cum inside me so badly, don't you, baby?"

"God, yes, Katie! I want to feel inside your pussy so badly."

Her kisses went from my mouth to my jaw line, nipping the side. She trailed kisses down my chest and licked the trail that led to my throbbing cock. She slid down the bed, wanting my cock once again. I was just going to have to wait a bit longer it seemed. The torture would be worth it.

She licked and sucked the tip of my cock teasingly. "You little devil you."

She was gorgeous as she lapped at my cock while looking me straight in the eyes. I was slowly losing my mind. She quickly climbed on my lap once again and moved above me, plunging my cock inside of her. She gasped above me, and I groaned in pleasure. I watched as she rode me slowly, moving on my cock in a torturously slow rhythm. Her red hair fell over her breasts as she bounced on my cock and I had the best view in the house. I put my hands on her hips and ground her onto me. Katie moaned like a kitten, and the sound drove me crazy. She tightened around my cock, and I knew she was about to spill around me. She came quite vocally, and I laughed, loving the sound of it.

"I love the sound of you cumming, Katie." She smiled down at me and rode me harder. She took my hand and sucked on my middle finger while she rode me hard. "Wow, baby, that is so hot."

She began to ride my cock harder, her body grinding into mine. The tension inside was building, and I was going to blow with her while she was in complete control over my orgasm. "Oh god, Katie, that feels so good." I came inside her hard, and she continued to rock on me, riding me to one of the most intense orgasms I'd ever had.

I was spent, and she felt wondrous on top of me. She bent forward and licked my mouth before kissing me hard. She climbed off and opened up a drawer to grab some Kleenex to clean off. Being with Katie had been amazing both times. It felt glorious being inside of her; despite the incredible orgasm I'd just had, I was a little sorry that it was over. I could smell her perfume around us as she climbed on my lap again and held me close to her.

"You smell fantastic, Katie."

"Thank you." She looked down into my eyes with a coy smile.

As I stared into her beautiful eyes, I couldn't help but wonder again how she'd been able to make it to the age of twenty-eight without ever having a man bring her to orgasm. "Can I ask you something personal?" I hoped she would indulge me and not think I was being rude—I had this urge to know more about her, and I was used to getting what I want.

She chuckled. "I'd say we're on more than personal terms at this point—and let me guess, you want to know about the orgasm thing?" I nodded and she continued. "You know, it's not for a lack of trying. I've had my share of partners, and most of our encounters were enjoyable, but I guess there was just something missing. A lack of intensity, I guess." She shrugged, and her smile widened. "Until now, that is."

I smiled back, feeling pretty flattered that she had enjoyed herself so much with me. Just thinking about it all made me want to go at it again, but I knew we had other things we should be doing instead. "Maybe we should consider getting to work."

"Maybe… That is a valid point, but I think I want to fuck you again." She gave me another huge smile, and I was lost.

If you want to continue reading this story,
you can get your copy from your favorite
vendor by searching for the title:

The Promise of Love
A Billionaire Romance

You can also find the e-book version by
typing this link in your computer's
browser:

https://www.hotandsteamyromance.com/products/the-promise-of-love-a-billionaire-romance

OTHER BOOKS BY THIS AUTHOR

Saving Her Rescuer: A Billionaire & A Virgin Romance

I was just trying to get away from my crazy ex for the weekend when I ended up in a giant pileup on the highway up to Gore Mountain.

https://geni.us/SavingHerRescuer

Sensual Sounds: A Rockstar Ménage

Lust. Lies. Double lives.

The rock and roll industry is full of people who are looking out for themselves and willing to do anything to rise to the top.

https://www.hotandsteamyromance.com/collections/frontpage/products/sensual-sounds-a-rockstar-menage

On the Run: A Secret Baby Romance

Murder. Lies. Fraud. Just another day in the lives of billionaires and women on the run.

https://www.hotandsteamyromance.com/collections/frontpage/products/on-the-run-a-secret-baby-romance

The Dirty Doctor's Touch: A Billionaire Doctor Romance

I am a master. An elitist. I am at the top of my field, and I know what I am doing.

https://www.hotandsteamyromance.com/collections/frontpage/products/the-dirty-doctor-s-touch-a-billionaire-doctor-romance

The Hero She Needs: A Single Daddy Next Door Romance

He's the only man I've ever wanted...

https://www.hotandsteamyromance.com/collections/frontpage/products/the-hero-she-needs-a-single-daddy-next-door-romance

You can find all of my books here:

Hot and Steamy Romance

https://www.hotandsteamyromance.com

Facebook

facebook.com/HotAndSteamyRomance

COPYRIGHT

©Copyright 2020 by Scarlett King - All rights Reserved

In no way is it legal to reproduce, duplicate, or transmit any part of this document in either electronic means or in printed format. Recording of this publication is strictly prohibited and any storage of this document is not allowed unless with written permission from the publisher. All rights are reserved. Respective authors own all copyrights not held by the publisher.

www.ingramcontent.com/pod-product-compliance
Lightning Source LLC
LaVergne TN
LVHW011717060526
838200LV00051B/2928